DRAGON STEEL

Laurence Yep

DRAGON STEEL

HARPER & ROW, PUBLISHERS

Dragon Steel

Copyright © 1985 by Laurence Yep

No part of this book may be
used or reproduced in any manner whatsoever without
written permission except in the case of brief quotations
embodied in critical articles and reviews.

Printed in the United States of America.

Harper & Row Junior Books, 10 East 53rd Street,
New York, N.Y. 10022. Published simultaneously in
Canada by Fitzhenry & Whiteside Limited, Toronto.

Library of Congress Cataloging in Publication Data
Yep, Laurence.

Dragon steel.

Summary: To free her clan from slavery at underwater
forges, the dragon princess Shimmer and her human
companion Thorn combat the Dragon King's jealousy and
treachery.

[1. Dragons—Fiction. 2. Fantasy] I. Title.
PZ7.Y44Dqn 1985   [Fic]   84-48338
ISBN 0-06-026748-8
ISBN 0-06-026751-8 (lib. bdg.)

Designed by Al Cetta
1 2 3 4 5 6 7 8 9 10
First Edition

To Jo,
who has already
traveled far

PROLOGUE

Thorn had saved the Princess's life,
Though only a human boy.
He'd stood beside her with his knife
And followed her with joy.

Monster and maze they did outwit,
Desert they did travel,
To catch the evil Civet
And break her wicked spell.

The Inland Sea was once so fair,
We dragons the noblest.
Our treasures were beyond compare,
Our kings and queens the proudest.

The Civet stole the Inland Sea
And took the shining flood.
And we lived on others' charity
Though it went against our blood.

Old Monkey knew all sorts of magic
Clever, clever Monkey
He bragged he'd catch Civet with a trick
And end her evil spree.

He drugged the Princess so she'd sleep
So he could hog the glory;
But he only made us dragons weep
At his treachery.

Monkey thought he was so wise.
He thought he was so clever.
But Civet saw through his disguise
And did him one trick better.

She loosed the waters of our home,
Upon a helpless city,
Leaving the Princess in the foam
With the mighty Monkey.

Then Civet changed into a mist
With the power of a stone.
Beyond the grasp of claw or fist,
She rose up all alone.

So Monkey flew to the dragons' ocean,
Not for pleasure, not for fun.
Into his head he'd gotten a notion
To "borrow" the High King's cauldron.

He'd boil away the water, was his boast,
And save the situation.
Among heroes he'd be the foremost.
He'd add to his reputation.

But the Princess and Thorn flew through the air
To slay or to be slain.
And Thorn tricked the witch within her lair
Into swallowing a chain.

Many a dragon would have hated.
Many a dragon killed.
Their anger could not go unsated,
Their vengeance unfulfilled.

But the Princess's anger left her heart
When she heard the Civet's story.
Instead she took Civet's part
And felt only pity.

So the Princess left the witch's mountain
With Thorn upon her back
And flying over the desert again,
She took the windy track.

To her clan she'd bring the news
And ask the High King for help.
She didn't think that he'd refuse
To restore our gardens of kelp.

—Popular dragon ballad
from *Singing to the Wind*

CHAPTER ONE

I was rehearsing my thank-you speech again when I felt the heat on my wings. It was too hot for the sun. No, it was magic—red-hot magic and strong too. So I forced myself to forget about the welcome banquet that the High King would give in our honor; and instead I concentrated on finding out what was wrong.

Of course, humans like Thorn don't feel such things so he just started to prompt me again. "Then you're supposed to say, 'As princess of the Inland Sea, I thank you for helping us regain our heritage.' "

"Hush. There's something wrong." I slowed the beating of my wings and looked below me toward Ramsgate, the capital of the humans. From far below, the watch began to sound the alarm on a gong; but I couldn't see anything wrong.

In fact, it would have been hard to find a more peaceful scene. The soft, hazy light of sunset made the buildings look like some dreamy picture drawn in chalk and ready to be washed away by the first rain. The towers and spires of Ramsgate rose like so many long, thin petals of a chrysanthemum; and the sandstone walls took on an almost rose, fleshy color.

"I don't see any bandits. It must be a fire in someone's kitchen." In his excitement, Thorn leaned over, shifting his position on my back.

I adjusted for the change in balance and then raised a paw, making sure that our sleeping prisoner was still tied securely to my back. The Witch, Civet, was our guarantee into the dragon kingdoms. "There aren't any bucket brigades, though."

Thorn's voice cracked with excitement. "No, there's the fire. It's rising almost like a fountain."

"Fountain?" I twisted my head around. Behind us, the sun was setting over the mountains.

"Over there on the hill." Thorn pointed toward our left. "Only it's gone now."

There was only one hill in Ramsgate and that

was off to my left where the palace of the King sat. Its great golden dome caught the evening sun so that it seemed to pulse like a red eye. Lights were being lit in its many rooms and the windows and doors glittered like the many eyes of some sea creature.

"Maybe it was just the reflection of the sun on the palace." But I began to beat my wings harder, eager to reach the safety of the dragon kingdoms that lay in the sea just ahead.

"There it is again," Thorn called.

I twisted my head around once more. The walls and towers of the palace seemed to shimmer as if some enormous fire were heating up the air. Suddenly a long, thin pillar of fire shot upward and then dissolved, sending tongues of magical fire flickering into the night like the seeds of a dandelion.

"What's that?" Thorn asked breathlessly.

I began to beat my wings even faster though I was a bit tired from our long journey. "I don't know and I'm not waiting to find out. Someone's working magic. Lie low on my neck so you don't provide any wind drag." I'd been so busy dreaming about all the banquets in my honor that I'd forgotten the first rule of survival: Always assume the worst.

"There's even more fire than before," Thorn cried.

The fire shot upward like the stalk of some giant seedling, rising, rising until it seemed to hit an invisible ceiling where it began to flatten. The flames licked outward and died, to reveal a gigantic bird with feathers that flickered now red, now yellow, like tongues of fire. Slowly, defiantly, it spread its wings over the palace; and the light went rolling over the golden dome.

"It's a flame bird." Someone was working magic for no apparent reason. I dove because I didn't feel like waiting around to see any more tricks. Tied about my neck was the mist stone that we'd taken from Civet. It would have let me change my body into a cloud of mist—if I had known the proper spell. But even if I could have used it, I wouldn't, because that would have left Thorn exposed.

The flat roofs of the houses seemed to leap up at me. A family having dinner on a rooftop flung themselves underneath the table and benches. Too late I saw the gleam of soldiers' armor on one rooftop. A flight of arrows was already hissing loudly up toward us. Though the Witch was tied to my back, the boy wasn't, so I couldn't bank sharply. All I could do was dive even lower into the narrow street itself. "Doesn't anything ever come easy for us?"

"Somehow we always manage to—" Thorn started to shout, and his words were lost in a gasp as we dropped within the street itself.

In the upper story windows human faces gaped at us like so many pink melons; and I winced as my left wingtip scraped against a stucco wall. But I didn't let myself panic. As my flying instructor said, there's only one name for fliers who make mistakes: corpses. Instead, I strained every muscle to pull up.

I managed to level off at two meters above the cobblestone street, and then I drew a shaky breath. "I don't understand it. Dragons have always been free to fly over Ramsgate before."

"Maybe they don't like tourists anymore." Thorn's arms and legs tightened around my neck. "Look out!"

I'd already seen the wagon filled with squashes and drawn in my paws. We just barely skimmed over its top; but my tail brushed the terrified driver backward. "Sorry," I called over my shoulder as squashes began cascading down onto the street. Then I swung my eyes forward again. "It's got to be team flying from now on," I told Thorn anxiously. "Keep your eyes on our rear."

Thorn was a game little creature and as brave a companion as I could ask for. "Okay. But if people here weren't mad before, they will be now. You'll get fined for reckless flying."

The air around us seemed to waver and I could feel a tremendous heat on the surface of my wings. Something magical was very close to me, and I thought I knew what it was. "At the moment, that's the least of our worries."

And I suddenly spread my wings out full to bring us to a sharp halt as I dropped to the street itself. My wingtips scraped themselves raw against the bricks of a wall and the cobblestones bumped and scraped my knees as we skidded along.

Some poor rag buyer stood in the center of the street with his two-wheeled handcart. He started to turn first to the left and then to the right as he tried to figure out a way to save his cart. But he hesitated too long. He had just enough time to leap backward before we plowed through the whole thing.

The cart's ancient boards splintered around us, and old clothes and rags went flying in a shower of cotton and wool. And then a large vest covered my eyes and I couldn't see anything.

"You're heading for a wall," Thorn yelled.

I never saw it, but I certainly felt it as my head jammed back against my neck.

I could only hear the shouts and screams dimly through the roaring noise that filled the air. It swelled in volume as if someone had decided to pour an entire river down on top of our heads. I tried to ask Thorn if he still had a good grip on me; but I couldn't hear my own voice.

And suddenly there was an explosion like a giant jar being flung against the ground, and there was a hissing noise like oil heating up in a thousand woks.

I plucked the vest from my face with one sore paw and saw small oil fires burning here and there on the street. Above them the flame bird was struggling to bring itself to a halt and turn for another dive at us. As it flapped its wings, a small feather fell from its breast to land on the street where it splattered and began burning.

From the long, trailing plumes of its tail to the tip of its sharp, pointed beak, it must have been four meters long, and its wings must have been some ten or more meters wide from wingtip to wingtip—far too big for the street. On the roofs of several houses, wherever its wings brushed, fires flickered into life and died just as quickly.

As large and deadly as it looked, it didn't seem to be particularly smart. In magic, bigger is not always better—unless you're trying to impress children. Any half-baked magician's apprentice can conjure up a large monster. It takes a real mage, though, to make it even half-intelligent.

Alarm gongs were beating all over the city now; and I didn't think they were for the flame bird but for us. I swung round. "I get the feeling that we're not wanted around here."

"Then maybe we should take the hint and leave," Thorn suggested.

"Yes, I think we should." With a great beat of my wings, I rose from the street. The reddening sky lay like a long, flat banner between the darkening house fronts. And it seemed to be a banner for freedom and for life; and I soared toward it.

I banked as slightly as I could over the rooftops. Arrows hissed at us from both sides of the street; but I flew low so that they clattered together harmlessly overhead.

Thorn's voice sounded strained—not from fear but from looking behind him. "The flame bird's in the air again."

I could feel the wave of heat rolling over the rooftops. "We're almost home," I told him. A half-kilometer ahead of us, I could see the wharves and cranes of the harbor. I beat my wings frantically, trying to head for the safety of the water.

As a child, on my way with my parents to visit my uncle, the High King, we had passed over the harbor. I remembered it as a busy place where dragons and humans had mixed together noisily and happily. But I was surprised when I saw the harbor now. Instead of being filled with round, tubby merchantmen, it was filled with long, sleek war galleys.

"Has everyone gone crazy?" I dove low so that we were sliding over the surface of the water. It hadn't been all that clean even when I was a child; but the water was now almost black with pitch and tar.

Thorn kicked his heel against the tough hide of my right side—not as an insult but for me to look in that direction. "I think the sailors have just declared war on us too."

A catapult thumped on one of the galleys and arrows rose in showers from the galley decks like clouds of angry mosquitos. My own tough hide gave me some protection, but the boy only had that soft human skin. "Take a breath," I yelled as I folded my wings and dove into the dirty water itself. I didn't have to worry about Civet. Her magic would protect her.

Water bubbled all around us from the force of our plunge, and I followed the little silver beads as they rose toward the surface. With a kick of my legs and a wriggle of my whole body I began to swim forward. I'd been heading straight for the harbor mouth before I went into the water. I could only hope I was still headed in the right direction now.

Overhead, arrows made sharp, gurgling sounds as they penetrated the surface, but the water stopped them within a few meters so that they halted and floated back to the surface like so many dead insects. Suddenly, something crashed into the water ahead of me, and I saw a boulder fall toward the harbor floor. Long chains of little bubbles streamed from the boulder's bottom. The humans must be using the catapults now. Another boulder crashed right above me and I barely twisted my head to the side in time. As it was the stone grazed my cheek.

I angled to my right with a sudden kick and then darted forward toward what I hoped was the harbor mouth. More boulders fell into the sea all around us. Frantically I tried to figure out how the humans were following us; and then I remembered the boy. They must be following his air bubbles.

He must have realized at the same time what was happening because suddenly I felt him let go of me. The little fool was going to sacrifice himself for me. I whirled around and saw him beginning to swim toward the surface; but I grabbed him by his scruffy collar and hugged him to my chest. We'd either get through this together or not at all.

At the moment, though, we would need speed, not guile, to get us out of this one. With a kick of my legs and a slash of my tail, I sent us up through the surface again. My wet wings now felt heavier;

but I forced them outward and brought them in sharply again so that we went shooting over the surface of the water. A few archers shot, but their arrows fell behind us. The catapults were being reloaded. I heard the twang of bow strings and I tensed, but they zipped into the water even farther behind me. We were now out of range of the archers.

I skimmed like a stone over the water toward the entrance to the harbor. A huge chain had been hung over its mouth as it would during wartime, and beneath it I could make out the heavy wire mesh of some net as well—as if the humans were afraid of some sea creature sneaking in. We would never have escaped underwater after all.

Suddenly, the water around us began to steam; and wavering over the surface of the water was the reflection of an object as bright as the sun. The flame bird had caught up with us again.

Behind me, I could hear Thorn take a deep breath as if he expected me to dive right away. "Not yet," I told him. I kept flying along as if I didn't see the light or feel the heat.

"Dive," Thorn yelled at me frantically. "It's getting close."

But I went on flying. Outside the harbor, the sea rose in swells so that sometimes my paws were splashing across the whitecaps. "How far away is it?"

"I guess a hundred meters," Thorn estimated.

"Tell me when it's twenty and then take a deep breath," I ordered.

He didn't cringe or whine like some other child might have. I was glad to have the boy not only as a partner but as a rider as well. "Eighty. What have you got planned?"

"You'll see." Everything would depend on timing.

"Right. Teamwork. It's sixty." Thorn was trying his best to sound calm but his voice broke with excitement. Still, I knew I could count on him.

It was almost as bright as day around us now.

"Forty." Thorn's voice was now a shrill yelp.

The reflected light of the flame bird glared up at us almost blindingly.

"Twenty." And I heard Thorn gasp as he took a deep breath.

I plunged into the water at an angle to the right of our original flight path. The water was already warm from the closeness of the flame bird, but the water began to boil now as the bird was almost on top of us. There was always the possibility that the bird wouldn't be able to halt its dive but go directly into the water; but I wasn't counting on it.

I broke the surface only ten meters from where the flame bird had halted in the air, beating its wings frantically and sending out gusts of heat.

When a sudden ocean swell swept underneath it, the water caught its claws. It gave a hollow screech—like someone screaming into a huge tube— as large bursts of steam rose. Almost instantly the magic fire spread back down its legs and over the claws; but in the brief moment the fire was out I could see that it had no flesh and blood at all, but only wires shaped like the outlines of claws.

I darted closer, sweeping my tail over the water so that I splashed a huge column of spray toward it. As a child playing with the other dragons, I had often done this; but I never thought my life would depend on it now. As the water drenched its left wing, the flames instantly disappeared in a cloud of steam, and it threw back its head to give a louder, more pained cry.

Deciding to take a chance, I dropped into the water only five meters away from it even as the wing burst back into life. The heat was almost blistering now, but spreading my wings and lashing my tail, I sent sheets of water at it. For a moment, its body was hidden in a huge ball of steam. Only its head was visible, twisting its way this way and that. But even though I couldn't see its body, I kept throwing water at it.

It tried to escape by rising into the air, but its steaming wings couldn't lift it. With a downward beat of my wings that slapped against the water, I rose into the air so that I was at the level of its chest. Spinning around, I swung my tail like a heavy club and felt it whip through the steam and crunch into hot, wet metal wires.

They broke with little screeches, and from all over the flame bird there were snapping noises. I swept my tail back and battered more wires. The left wing went spinning with a splash into the water. I could see its wiry outline before it sank.

The flames of its head suddenly shot into the air and then gathered into a ball that darted like a frightened bird back toward the palace. All that was left was the wire skeleton of a bird with a broken chest and one wing missing. And even as I watched, it toppled backward into the water.

CHAPTER TWO

I looked at the bubbling surface of the water where the wire frame was sinking. "I wish I knew what was going on."

Thorn patted my neck comfortingly. "We were in the wilderness for a long time."

I drifted in a slow, thoughtful circle through the air. "Maybe I ought to disguise myself as a human and do some checking."

Thorn adjusted his grip. "During a war, people don't take kindly to a stranger asking questions."

He had a point. I swung around toward the east. The sky was a deep violet color and the sea on the horizon was black; but I could just make out the patch of land about a hundred meters square. "Well, we're right over the Citadel. We should find a dragon garrison there."

"Where is it?" Thorn inquired curiously. "All I see is that scruffy little island."

I rose higher so I could get above the wind currents that wanted to carry us back toward land. "Don't judge things just from the surface." Actually, it wasn't a bad philosophy in general. "That 'scruffy island' is just the tip of a huge mountain that rises for more than a kilometer from the side of the continent."

It was odd that I didn't see dragons; but since no flame birds or arrows or boulders came up at us from the island, I assumed it was still in our hands. I dropped down in a spiral—ready to fly away at the first sign of trouble.

There was a large dome on top of carved marble pillars in the center of the island surrounded by a grove of trees. From the leeward side of the island extended a half-dozen wharves for customs inspection. A tax was levied on the cargo of each human ship before it used the sea lanes to cross the dragon kingdoms; but the wharves were empty now.

It wasn't quite the entrance that I'd planned for myself. I had expected to stop on a nearby beach and groom both myself and Thorn. Instead, here

I was plopping down with scraped knees and burnt wings.

Almost immediately over two dozen of the columns began to waver, shifting from black-veined marble into dragons rearing on their hind legs. Around the neck of the first dragon was the steel disk with the double concentric circle of a lieutenant.

It had been centuries since I had last spoken to another dragon so Thorn and I had carefully worked out a greeting. "Good news—" I began.

But the lieutenant interrupted me. "Are those two humans brisoners?" He didn't distinguish between his *b*'s and *p*'s so I knew he was from the southern seas. But I'd heard his arrogant tone among humans as well as among dragons. He was a young pup so impressed with his title and duties that he'd puffed himself up. Well, he'd come down a little once he knew who I was.

"The woman is." I reached a paw over my shoulder and caught Thorn by the collar. "The boy is a companion."

The lieutenant dropped to all fours and his soldiers copied him. "No dragon would call a human friend now. The borders and the sea lanes have been closed."

So the dragons and humans weren't at war exactly; but anyone trespassing over the other's space would be attacked—as we had been. "I've been traveling deep in the interior of the land. It takes a while for word to reach inland."

"Identify yourself. Who are you and what is your clan?" The soldiers were fanning out in a crescent, ready to pounce on me at the first sign of trouble. It was a far cry from the triumphant entrance Thorn and I had planned.

"Let me do the talking," I whispered to Thorn, and set him down on his feet.

"I'm ready if that doesn't work." He put his hand instead on the hilt of the kitchen knife that was stuck through the rag that he used as a sash. He was a brave enough soul, but it would be futile against a dragon's claws.

Though it had been centuries since my etiquette lessons, I drew myself up as grandly as any queen. "I am Shimmer of the Inland Sea; and a princess of the royal blood." But I was mistaken if I thought my title and ancestry would awe him.

The lieutenant merely curled up his lip scornfully. "And I thought we'd seen the last of your kind."

I guess that I had been expecting everyone to

behave as if we were in some chivalric poem where everyone is courteous and noble. What he needed was a lesson in manners. I lifted my head even higher and looked at him from under haughty eyelids. "How dare you address me in such a rude manner?"

The lieutenant's eyes raked me from snout to tail. "Brincesses of the royal blood don't carry around bassengers like a donkey."

I suppose having Thorn and Civet on my back made for a less than regal picture. Even so, I maintained my majestic pose while I tried to explain with solemn dignity, "I have been in exile."

The lieutenant suddenly clicked the claws of one paw against the marble floor. "I once heard of a Shimmer who was outlawed by her own clan."

I almost let my shoulders droop; but I caught myself in time. I couldn't get away from my past even now. Still, I decided to brazen it out. If my title and appearance didn't gain me respect, my deeds should. "I am she," I said, and waved a paw regally toward Civet. "But I've captured the witch Civet so our homeland can be restored."

I waited for the other dragons to jump and do back flips in the air; but they didn't even smile.

Instead, the lieutenant let out a loud, braying laugh. "Assuming that the humans would let you travel across their lands, who would bay for restoring your homeland? Go away. We don't want any more beggars, royal or otherwise."

"You're refusing to admit me?" My jaw dropped open in angry disbelief.

The lieutenant jerked a claw impatiently toward the human lands. "An outlaw is supposed to stay away from other dragons."

I tried to think of something else to say. Once I reached the palace, I was certain that the High King, Uncle Sambar, would lift the outlawry decree. But I had to get past this young pup first.

I wasn't sure what to do, but it was Thorn who came to my rescue this time. He refused to back down before the haughty lieutenant. "Even when we can tell you about the harbor defenses and the flame bird?"

"Flame bird?" The lieutenant drew his eyebrows together in puzzlement and looked with new interest at my burns and scrapes. Apparently, the flame bird was some new trick the humans had just worked up.

Thorn folded his arms. He was a much shrewder

bargainer than I was. "Do you think we're going to tell a flunky about something that important?"

The lieutenant sat down on his haunches and stroked his chin suspiciously. "Why would a human betray his own kind?"

"Because"—Thorn glanced at me—"Her Highness here has been a better friend than any human."

I put a foreleg around Thorn's shoulder to show that I valued his company too. "We'll report only to Uncle Sambar, the High King."

The lieutenant started to turn to his soldiers. "I'll have to consult with the balace."

I tilted my head forward and fixed my eyes on his challengingly. We had him now, and I wasn't going to let up. "And what will you say when flights of flame birds attack you?"

"But to go directly to the High King?" The young lieutenant seemed shocked at the boldness of the idea.

"You don't have much to lose," I coaxed him. "But you've got a lot to gain if my news is as special as I think it is."

The lieutenant glanced from me to the human lands, though they were lost in the darkening twilight. He wasn't nearly as roosterish as before.

In fact, he sounded almost frightened. "I don't know."

"If you want to be stuck in some outpost all your life, go on." I spread my wings and flapped them lightly as if I were warming up to fly away. "But you won't ever get another opportunity like this."

That seemed to decide him. He pointed to another dragon. "Sergeant, you'll be in charge of the blatoon. I'll take a squad to escort the"—he paused as he hunted for the right word—"the Brincess to her uncle."

"I'll need a breathing pearl for the boy," I said quickly.

"You can't mean to take one of the enemy into the sea," the lieutenant sputtered indignantly.

Thorn held up a hand before I could explode. "It's all right." He gave me another one of his brave smiles. "I don't want to keep you from seeing your home."

I looked at the small, ragged and now slightly singed boy. He'd been willing to sacrifice himself in the harbor; and apparently he was willing to do almost the same thing again. I might not be able to match his loyalty, but I had to try. I couldn't abandon him now. "You don't get away from me that easily. We're a team."

"A dragon and a boy?" The lieutenant looked disgusted.

"You can think what you like," I warned him, "but that's the way it is." Though I hated to miss the dragon kingdoms when I was so close, I was prepared to fly away if that's what it took to keep my partner.

Apparently the chance of a promotion meant more to the lieutenant than his own sensibilities. "Get a bearl," the lieutenant snapped to one of his soldiers.

The soldier trotted over to the grove of trees and slipped her claw into a hole in the trunk of one of them. Lifting out a small leather pouch, she opened it and poured out a half-dozen pearls— each of which hung from a leather thong. Taking one between her claws, she put the rest back into the pouch and returned it to the tree trunk. She would have brought it to the lieutenant, but he motioned for her to bring it directly to us.

I took it from her, inspecting the small blue-silver bead. It looked like a breathing pearl, but I made a note to take the descent slowly just in case.

"Here." I presented it to Thorn. "Put this on; and whatever happens, don't lose it."

Thorn lifted it from my paw. "Or I'll drown?"

I lowered my paw. "Yes, but with the pearl, you'll be able to breathe just as you would on the land. And the pearl will also keep you warm when we go into the lower depths—they can get pretty cold; and you'll be protected against the water pressure."

"I'll be careful then." Thorn hung it around his neck.

I looked over his head toward the lieutenant. "We're ready."

As the lieutenant led us to one side of the citadel's top, he pointed toward Civet. "Won't she need a bearl too?"

"No, she's magical." I paused on the edge as the water foamed around the steep side. The darkening sea now looked slick and black as obsidian. As a precaution, I took hold of Thorn's collar.

"Can't you find a better way to hold me?" he complained. "You make me feel like a pet kitten."

"If the collar breaks, you just lose some cloth." I watched as three dragons kicked themselves into the air, arching like eels into the water with hardly a splash at all. "But if I hold you by the arm and that breaks—well, that will take considerably more repair."

"Brincess." The lieutenant bowed ironically and motioned us to go. I couldn't wait to reach Uncle Sambar and have him wipe that smirk from the lieutenant's face.

"Keep your mouth closed for the first few minutes," I warned Thorn, and, folding my wings, I gave a little kick and went slipping into the water.

CHAPTER THREE

Though I couldn't see the other three dragons, I could feel their legs kick at the water as they closed around us. And then we were swimming away from the cloud of silvery bubbles that we had raised.

The lieutenant with three other dragons followed almost immediately, their bodies lost in bubbly columns that quickly dissolved into a cloud from which they emerged.

I guess the pearl worked all right because the next moment Thorn was staring below us at the dim mountain's straight lines. "You're right. It really is a mountain. It's funny, though. It didn't look like much before."

"Not everything is what it seems," I said simply.

Thorn's long hair flowed like tongues of black fire around his head as he craned his neck forward. "It's so dark that it's spooky—like there's nothing beneath us."

The lieutenant snickered. "You're welcome to go back."

It was one thing for me to make fun of Thorn, but quite another for a stranger. "I've had just about enough of your insults." Letting go of the boy, I flipped over the lieutenant's head and flicked my claws over his scales lightly with a rasping sound.

The lieutenant whirled around, claws outstretched as if he would have liked nothing better than to challenge me. The water swirled as his squad took up positions above and below and around me. "I don't think you understand, *Brincess*," he said with a sneer. "We aren't your escort; we're your guards."

My claws itched to teach this young pup a lesson; but I had to remind myself that princesses didn't brawl like alley cats. They let their uncle Sambar, the High King, punish his underlings for them. So I contented myself with raising my head defiantly. "I'd like to see you survive a desert the way this boy has." The idea of any place without water made that snippy officer shift uneasily.

"He did?" the lieutenant asked doubtfully.

"And more." I turned my attention back to Thorn as if that was all the conversation the lieutenant deserved. Though it was dark this far down, I thought Thorn's face seemed red with embarrassment. I'd have to do what I could to make him feel better. "This is the edge of the continent. Where the land ends, the sea kingdoms begin." I gestured at the slope. "We call this the Rim because the ocean is like a giant bowl."

The lieutenant's voice rose insolently. "This way, Princess." And he swung us into a current that flowed toward the east.

I looked at Thorn who was beginning to flail clumsily at the water. "Better climb on, boy," I sighed to him. "I don't think there's going to be any rest for us tonight."

The lieutenant stared in disbelief. "You'd let a human ride you again?"

Thorn hovered near my neck, afraid to climb on. "We're a team," I explained simply, "and this little rider helped me destroy a flame bird." Reaching up a paw, I grabbed Thorn's collar and swung him around behind me so he could sit on my shoulders just behind my neck. But a green light suddenly outlined the motion of my foreleg.

"What made that light?" Thorn asked in an awed voice.

"We call it the season of fire," I explained. It had been so long since I'd been in the dragon kingdoms that I'd almost forgotten all about it. "And I don't think there's ever a lovelier time in the ocean. There are tiny creatures called plankton that rise toward the surface at night, and they give off a bright light." And I raised a claw and traced my name in the water.

"This is fun." Thorn began to draw a face in the water. It hovered like ghostly fire.

"If you don't mind." The lieutenant lashed his tail and it swept a huge patch of fire through the water.

"Keep your eyes open during the ride, boy. You'll really see something then." And, with an arching of my back, I sent myself charging after the lieutenant.

I think the lieutenant deliberately set a hard pace for me despite the load I carried. But at first, I was enjoying myself too much to notice. As the plankton rose more thickly about us, our bodies began to carve trails of fire behind us. "If we had the time," I panted to Thorn, "we could use the whole sea for our canvas and trace lines all over it."

"I've never seen anything like it," Thorn murmured delightedly. I twisted my head around on my neck and saw that he was holding on with only one arm while he had raised the other, watching the cold light flickering like flames from his forearm.

And as we swam on, it seemed as if we were moving not through the ocean, but through the heart of a black sun that marked our paths with a bright but cold light.

It had been a long while since I had swum this much, and I began to feel aches in muscles that I'd forgotten I'd had. But I was determined to keep up with the other dragons. And so I forced my legs to kick and my body to undulate long after I wanted to quit. Every now and then the lieutenant would sneak a glance at me to see if I was tiring; but I would make a point of swimming even more strongly.

And as the squad began to swim more sluggishly, I saw grudging respect on their faces, but the lieutenant only seemed to become angrier when he saw he wasn't going to beat me. Behind me, I could hear Thorn begin to snore, and I lifted one leg and rested a paw on him so that he would not fall off. But that made swimming all the harder.

Still, I've always been the stubborn one. It's gotten me into trouble more times than I like to remember; but I wasn't about to give in now. One by one, members of the squad began to weary from the pace and drop behind us until there was only the lieutenant and myself.

Finally, the lieutenant slowed, paddling his legs stiffly at the water. "You're in better condition than I thought," he panted.

I made a point of swimming a few strokes beyond him. "I've wandered all over the human lands and endured a good deal of trouble. It would take more than a young egotistical fool to make me quit."

The lieutenant glided along. "But I still can't get over the boy."

"I told you. He's a friend." And when the lieutenant just stared at me in puzzlement, I added, "You've lived most of your life among your own kind. You don't know what it's like to be alone. When that happens, you learn to value a good heart when you find one."

He studied me for a long time as if he still couldn't make me out; but finally he just shrugged. "Well, I just hobe I never have to find out."

We swam along more slowly while the rest of his squad caught up to us. Since he seemed in a better mood, I asked him, "How long have things been bad between the dragons and humans?"

The lieutenant moved along with an easy, wriggling motion. "Just in the last few months when their king, the Butcher, began to demand all sorts of things on the Rim. He wants to send boats outside of the usual sea lanes and he wants to increase his quota of fish. All sorts of mad things. Even factories on the beach."

It seemed that the Butcher had become rather impatient with trade treaties that had existed for centuries between humans and dragons. He wanted his human fishers to be able to drop their nets wherever they wanted instead of in designated areas; and he wanted free access to the sea instead of keeping his ships to the sea lanes.

"That's all a dragon needs," I snorted. "There

you are, floating peacefully on your back and the next thing you know some merchant ship is trying to moor itself to your snout."

One of the younger dragons in the group shook his head. "I don't see how he's going to win any war, though. We can travel up the rivers and into the land, but it's going to be hard for him to fight us in the sea. All we have to do is dive down."

"I've heard a lot about him in my travels. He must have some trick up his sleeve," I warned. "He's as callous as his name, but he's no fool. He's yet to lose any war that he's fought."

The lieutenant frowned. "The strange thing is that the humans know exactly where to go when they want to create an incident. He seems to have a detailed knowledge of the dragon kingdoms—even down to the guard posts."

But the young dragon was too sure of himself to know any better. "This is still one war that he'll lose."

"The Butcher seems to think otherwise," the lieutenant snapped, and went on describing each new incident—culminating recently when some human war galleys had left the sea lanes when no one was watching and had gone straight to the palace, where they had proceeded to drop a load of garbage. It was at that point that Sambar had ordered the borders closed.

As the sun began to rise, a soft light began to slip through the water; and I could see the first of the seamounts begin to glow in the distance. They were mountains that had thrust themselves up slowly from the dark sea floor into the light. And then the tops had collapsed, creating flat areas just within the regions of sunlight so coral could grow.

But generations had transformed the seamounts into one long continuous garden. They had lovingly planted sea anemones and lilylike tube worms; and coral and sponges had been formed into multicolored hedges and trees.

And as the light swept the sides of the seamounts, coral worms on long, stiff stalks began to thrust petaled mouths outward into the water. And the anemones began to uncurl. Because of the twilight, they seemed to be materializing from the water like ghosts. Fish began to swirl in bright, colored clouds over the gardens, and in the distance I could hear a sea lizard begin its chirruping.

I couldn't think of a better moment to see the palace for the first time. "Wake up, boy." And I shook Thorn.

"Huh, what?" he asked sleepily.

"We're at the palace." I slowed for a moment so he could take in the view.

At the heart of the ring of seamounts, mountains rose close together like the fingers of giant hands reaching out of the shadows for the light; but these were fingers tattooed with living light—coral worms and other animals that gave a soft glowing light so that the mountains seemed to be ringed with gemlike fires. They almost reached the surface.

The smallest of the mountains was perhaps five hundred meters wide; and there were some that seemed to be several kilometers in circumference, and they were honeycombed with caves. But the largest mountain was a squat giant whose sides had been intricately carved for a hundred generations until the rock itself seemed alive with all the strange creatures that the dragons had met. Some sections showed dragons battling one another, or perhaps dancing. In other areas, ledges and terraces had been carved from the rock so that parts of the mountain seemed to be made of the finest lace.

"Where's the palace?" Thorn asked eagerly. "Behind that ridge of mountains?"

The lieutenant laughed. "The balace *is* that ridge

of mountains." And with a quick command, the lieutenant ordered his squad about us, and we swam in formation toward the palace and my destiny.

CHAPTER FOUR

The High King was already holding audience when we were ushered into the throne room. Above us the ceiling soared upward for a half kilometer to form a rounded dome in the center of which was a hole shaped like a four-pointed star. Crystal windows, also in the shape of stars, had been set in the dome to correspond to the stars of the night sky; but the dome itself had been covered with bright, sapphire-colored coral worms so that the audience room seemed to be covered with a living, moving sky. And once the sun had set, the worms would retreat into their jet-black tubes so that the audience room would be covered by blackness at night. Then night-feeding worms would appear like stars.

During all those long years of wandering among

humans, I had known I would return to my own kind some day—even if I hadn't been sure of how. It wouldn't be long now before I would reclaim my proper place among dragons.

I lifted my head and arched my back haughtily as I had been taught at my mother's court—and almost bumped into a gaping Thorn as he halted right under one of the many ornate archways. Our escort would have churned right over him if I hadn't blocked their way.

Thorn's mouth dropped open. "It's big enough for a city."

Dragons all around us began to turn to stare at Thorn. Their scales had been polished until they were almost like old jade; but their claws had only been given a thin coating of gold paint or even just yellow so I knew these were only ordinary petitioners and the usual sort of hangers-on that you find at court. Many of them scowled at Thorn while others smirked.

That showed what they knew about a true friend. There was more courage and loyalty in that boy's little finger than they had in their entire bodies. I leaned over, not caring what they thought of my talking to a human. "A small city, though. It's only a kilometer square. And there are probably no more than five thousand dragons here."

Thorn's head jerked round in the direction of a snicker. "Oh," he said in a small voice—as if he were suddenly afraid of embarrassing himself.

I made a point of hooking a paw under his arm and kept it there despite the shocked whispers and pointing claws. "This whole room," I explained, ignoring the other dragons, "was carved from the mountain at the time of Sambar the Destroyer over fourteen hundred years ago."

"Don't dawdle. His Most Exalted Majesty is waiting for you." With immense self-importance, the lieutenant tried to shove me along as if I were a runaway cow. I couldn't wait for him to get his comeuppance. In a matter of moments, I would no longer be an outlaw but a welcome member of the court.

I pulled Thorn in protectively against me and twisted slightly to let the lieutenant past. "Then tell this tangle of worms to let us through."

But the name of the High King was enough to make the nearby dragons make way before the lieutenant could do anything. A murmur swept through the crowd, and dragons further away began rearing up on their hind legs to see what all the excitement was about.

It was like watching a mole tunnel through the earth—but in reverse—as the lane opened up among curious, scaled dragons.

The lieutenant brushed past us as he hurriedly buffed his claws against his chest. It made a sound like a knife edge being stropped against leather. "Make way," he ordered, even though it was no longer necessary. "Make way."

"This is no worse than chasing Civet inside her own mountain," I whispered reassuringly to Thorn; and then, letting go of the boy, I began to follow the lieutenant.

The sunlight fell soft and green through the windows in the great dome so that it seemed as if the dome itself were supported by hundreds of slender pillars of light around platforms at the center of the audience room.

The lowest platform was for dragon mages, officers and other court functionaries. It was set off by a brass rail and covered with brass ornaments on polished granite. The next platform was for nobility and it had a silver rail and silver ornaments on white marble.

Above that was a platform of black marble and gold for those of the royal blood. The family of the High King would sit there along with the other dragon rulers when they attended the High King.

Finally, in the center of the black platform was a flat, circular dais carved from a gigantic piece of jade.

Thorn was looking in the same direction as I was. "What are the decorations carved on the side of the dais?" Thorn whispered.

"The four symbols of dragon power." I ticked them off on my claws. "The bowl, mirror, cloud and pearl." They had been chiseled along the circular sides and framed by crashing waves.

I'm afraid that as children, my brother and I had compared the dais to a giant head of lettuce—a reference that most of the court dragons had not understood since they had never been on the land; and their bewilderment had only added to our amusement.

And there, some twenty meters above the floor of the audience room floor, was my uncle, Sambar XII, in all his glory. The bowl and mirror would be locked away in the deepest, most secret vaults; but he was wearing the rainbow pearl on his forehead, casting a soft glow over his body, and the cloud plaque of the first High King, Calambac the Swift, hung on a gold chain around his neck.

Of smoke jade, the plaque had been carved in the shape of a rain cloud to recall the time when many suns burned the earth and Calambac had to destroy all but one with rain clouds he had carried up on his back.

But all the magnificence and pomp in the world couldn't change what Uncle Sambar was—a worm lolling around on a head of lettuce.

While Thorn and I knelt, the lieutenant was whispering to some minor court official who in turn whispered to someone else. In all a dozen whispers were exchanged before a dragon with a voice as deep and rumbling as thunder announced, "Your Most Exalted Majesty, Sambar the Strong, here is the outlaw, Shimmer."

We had already been through so much together that I wasn't going to act as if I were ashamed of our partnership. I glanced at Thorn and then looked back up. "And friend," I shouted out in a loud, clear voice. We might as well let the entire palace know what the situation was.

The big-voiced dragon looked a bit put out that

I hadn't sent my correction to him first. "And friend," he grunted sulkily.

Uncle Sambar raised his head. "You must be our niece. Even if your wanderings had changed your features, we would have known that exquisite sense of decorum anywhere."

This was my big moment. *Now* that lieutenant would be sorry for his insolence. With a joyful kick, I rose in the water so that the entire court could see me announce my news. "I bring you great news. The Witch, Civet, has been captured and the Inland Sea is free to be restored." I thought that at least some folk would cheer, so I was surprised by the silence. "Well," I muttered to myself, "don't wear yourselves out rejoicing." I looked around me but all I saw were the same scornful expressions that the lieutenant had worn when I had first announced my identity.

Uncle Sambar merely lifted a languid hand and a servant instantly raised a golden bowl from which he selected a leathery turtle's egg—almost purple from the vinegary gel it had soaked in. "Is that what's attached to your back? We thought you were growing another head."

The royal dragons tittered about him, and the

titter became a chuckle among the nobles and open laughter by the time it reached the lowest platform and spread through the audience room. This wasn't going at all the way I had imagined.

"Keep your temper," Thorn cautioned from below.

Even if Thorn hadn't been there, I would have known that this was one of the few situations in which pride was a luxury. I still needed Uncle Sambar's help if not his friendship.

"I have come to ask your aid in restoring my homeland and the glory of my clan. Civet loosed the waters of the Inland Sea in another place. We need Baldy's magical cauldron. With it, we might be able to transport the water back to its original site."

Uncle Sambar popped the egg into his mouth and crunched it enthusiastically. I could see the rolls of fat around his haunches and thighs. He shouldn't have been called Sambar the Strong but Sambar the Fat. "But we have heard how resourceful you are."

I tried to keep my voice warm and hopeful. "But with appropriate safeguards, I was hoping your mages could use the cauldron to—"

The servant held up the bowl again, but Uncle Sambar dismissed him with a wave of his hand. "In case you hadn't noticed on your way here, we have broken off relations with the human kingdom."

"But surely someone with your wisdom and experience can resolve this crisis." I bowed my head once. "And then we can think of more peaceful things—like restoring my home."

Uncle Sambar motioned to another servant who plumped some pillows for His Exalted Majesty to lay his head on. "No doubt. But there was talk of a flame bird."

"Yes," I said, and told him briefly of our fight with the flame bird. Uncle Sambar's generals seemed more interested than my uncle in my description of the harbor and how I destroyed the flame bird itself with water.

Uncle Sambar flicked his tail in a leisurely circle. "Our dearest niece, you don't really expect us to believe this. You must have used the pearl."

I floated there for the whole court to see—and feeling like a bloated sausage that everyone was going to laugh at. I'd been so caught up in my daydreams that I'd let myself forget just how greedy Uncle Sambar could be. He could have cared less about what I had done or what I needed.

I could forget about teaching a lesson to insolent lieutenants and courtiers. In fact, I had been a fool to think that I could ever be a princess again. I'd be lucky to get out of the palace with what I had brought in.

"Pearl?" I tried to look as innocently puzzled as I could. But looking up at Uncle Sambar reminded me of that time long ago when my brother had first accused me of taking it—only there wasn't going to be any easy escape now. While my brother's guards hadn't expected a fight, Uncle Sambar's were watching my every move.

"The dream pearl that you stole." Uncle Sambar slowly sat up again. "You were outlawed for that theft, or had you forgotten that little detail?"

It was hidden under a fold of flesh on my forehead, but I wasn't about to admit it to that load of blubber. "I didn't steal it. It was mine. My mother left it to me, not to my brother." My eyes searched the black marble platform. "Where is Pomfret anyway?"

Uncle Sambar laced his paws together over his gross belly. "Vanished one day. No one knows where."

There was more than my uncle was telling me.

"And the nobles of my clan? I don't see any of them here."

Uncle Sambar twiddled his hind paws. "They serve me at various faraway outposts—like the loyal subjects they are." He added meaningfully, "And as you should."

After being outlawed for taking the dream pearl, I wasn't about to give it up easily. Hastily I began to untie the knots binding Civet to my back. "But I've brought you a marvelous gift—a Witch who knows all sorts of magic. All your mages have to do is remove the chain that she swallowed."

Uncle Sambar motioned several of the mages to take Civet. They rose and lifted her from my back. "We thank you for your gift, but I can hardly put her on a chain and wear her around my throat."

"But I also have another present for you: the fabled mist stone." I undid the mist stone and handed it to a mage who passed it on to the Grand Mage. "It will let the wearer turn himself or herself into mist."

When the oval-shaped jewel was passed up to him, Uncle Sambar fondled it lovingly. "Ah, how exquisite." I was wrong, though, when I hoped that it would buy off Uncle Sambar. "We thank you, dearest niece. But there is still the dream pearl."

Suddenly the lieutenant darted forward and his claws closed round Thorn's neck. His other paw trapped Thorn's hands. "She values the boy, Your Exalted Majesty. I think he's some kind of pet."

"I am not a pet. Let go of me." Thorn began to kick at the lieutenant—with little success.

Outraged, I glared at Uncle Sambar. I was wrong to call him Sambar the Fat. He was Sambar the Worm. "Is this the justice that your people can expect?"

Uncle Sambar folded his two forepaws together over his round belly. "If we were concerned with justice, you would have been dead a long time ago. You are still an outlaw, after all. It is death to approach other dragons. We are really being quite merciful."

I shook my head insistently, hoping that I might appeal to some bit of kingly pride. "Uncle Sambar, you can't really mean to use a human child."

Uncle Sambar looked about the dragons thronged below. "Do I hear any objections?"

The other dragons were silent. They had no reason to anger the High King for a stranger. I had been fooling myself all those years that I had assumed being a princess really meant something. It had only been a title—mere sounds. What counted was my one friend.

I looked at the lieutenant. He could crush Thorn's spine just by closing his paw. I knew I shouldn't risk it—but maybe I could work one little bit of magic. I pretended to let my shoulders sag in defeat. "Very well."

Uncle Sambar unclasped his forepaws and waved a claw grandly toward the lieutenant. "Well, done, lieutenant. You are hereby promoted to my guard immediately."

"No," Thorn called out angrily.

I let my head droop for a moment as if the weight of the world were suddenly on my back; but I was secretly murmuring the spell and moving my claws ever so slightly in a magical sign. I did not know the secrets of casting the large, numerous illusions as my mother had; but perhaps I could cast a small one.

But I hadn't reckoned with Thorn. The injustice was too much for him to bear. "The pearl is hers," Thorn shouted to Uncle Sambar. "You've no right to do this."

I stared at Thorn in disbelief. So did Uncle Sambar. He was sitting on the dais as if Thorn had just dropped a boulder on top of his Most Exalted skull. No one ever talked to Uncle Sambar about any rights except his. He sucked in his breath sharply and reared upward as if Thorn had just used the filthiest word Sambar had ever heard—and perhaps Thorn had. There were times when I could have wished Thorn were less feisty.

"Rights? What rights?" The Most Exalted voice rose shrilly. "Everything within this sea is ours!"

He looked like he would have ordered Thorn's death with his very next breath if I hadn't dropped down and lightly tapped the side of his head. "Shut up," I hissed at the boy. I tried to arch an eyebrow to warn him that I was up to something, but he missed my meaning completely.

He rubbed the sore spot with righteous indignation. "But I was just trying to help you."

"It has to be this way." I pretended to scowl at the boy before I spun around once again to face Uncle Sambar. "Never mind the boy. He's been raised among hairless apes. What does he know about manners?" For that matter, what did Uncle Sambar? But of course, I didn't say that. I just put my paw up to the fold of the flesh.

The dream pearl seemed to tingle when my claws touched it—almost as if it were sharing the joke with me. My mother had once told me that the dream pearl could be willful in its own way. I could feel it pulse there against my forehead as if the pearl itself were laughing as I extracted the fake pearl.

Its light flickered in silvery rainbow colors around the audience room; and there were admiring murmurs even from the mages who were used to all sorts of wonders. But then there was never quite as lovely a magic as that of the dream pearl—fake or otherwise. I handed it to a dragon mage who passed it on to another mage until it reached the Grand Mage himself—a dragon.

My stomach did little flipflops as he grasped it eagerly in his claw. But he didn't seem to notice that it was an illusion.

I was sure now that we could leave the audience chambers and make our escape with the real dream pearl. We ought to have at least a few hours before my uncle finished holding his audience and tried out his new treasure—only to find out that I had given him an illusion instead.

But though Thorn had a good heart, I couldn't say the same for his head. As soon as the lieutenant had released the boy, the would-be hero pulled out his old kitchen knife. Compared to a dragon's claws and teeth, I suppose no one had considered the kitchen knife dangerous enough to take it away from him.

"No, you little fool." Desperately I tried to block him with my body.

But with that clumsy kick he tried to paddle past me toward the first mage. "Give that back to her," he ordered fiercely.

I wrapped a leg around the boy and lifted him kicking and squirming in the water. "Drop that!" And I snatched the kitchen knife from his hand and threw it with a clank onto the floor. Then I appealed to Uncle Sambar. "He didn't mean it."

But the damage to the Most Exalted dignity had already been done. Uncle Sambar rose so that the dais creaked under the sudden shift of his kingly bulk. "How dare he threaten us. Take those fools and put them into the deepest of our dungeons."

Most of the time, I valued Thorn's courage; but sometimes it definitely had its drawbacks.

CHAPTER FIVE

Guards with gold-tipped claws and helmets with plumelike worms dragged us down gloomy corridors where the only light came from red coral worms that grew in patches every fifteen meters. I could just make out the marks of the chisels that had carved the corridor from the solid stone; but the deeper we went the cruder the work became until we were moving through what seemed like a natural tunnel to which cells had been added.

Thorn glanced apologetically over his shoulder at me. "Don't worry. We'll get out of this. We always do."

I suppose I should have been proud of Thorn for defying an entire palace; but at the moment, I was feeling more upset with him over spoiling our escape. "We'd better," I muttered, "considering that it was a team effort that put us here." And then I turned to the Grand Mage. "I don't understand. My clan always used to be so welcome at the palace."

The Grand Mage, who was leading the way, was one of those creatures who are most delighted when they have someone to lord it over. "You had a homeland then. When your clan came to His Most Exalted Majesty, they only had what they could carry."

I could feel the rage rise inside me—not for myself but for my clan. "And whatever happened to kindness?"

The Grand Mage gave a haughty toss of his head. "We couldn't feed beggars indefinitely. Everyone was put to work."

During all my imaginings, I had never considered the most obvious possibility. Mercy and charity belong to pleasant little tales—not to real life. All these years, I had forgotten the second rule for survival: Always be realistic; daydreams can get you killed. "I wish my uncle wasn't giving us such special treatment."

"Don't you like it?" the Grand Mage asked insolently. "There's only one other prisoner who gets to enjoy such hospitality."

I drifted for a moment. "Who is it? My uncle's interior decorator?"

The Grand Mage used his tail to lash me along. "No, a thief who's tried his tricks once too often."

"Thief?" I glanced at Thorn and then back at the Grand Mage. "He wouldn't happen to be covered in yellow fur, would he?"

"You know Monkey?" I could see that I had just gone even lower in his judgment.

"Her Highness has had to associate with all sorts of people in her travels." Thorn bumped into a wall and slid along its slippery surface as the passage took an unexpected turn.

I thought of all the times when, disguised as a human, I'd had to huddle with beggars just to stay warm. If the Grand Mage knew just what I'd done to stay alive, he probably wouldn't even talk to me. "Yes," I said drily, "but I wouldn't call Monkey a friend—more like an associate." While Thorn and I had gone after Civet, Monkey had come after the cauldron to remove the water from the city that Civet had flooded.

"I guess he's not as good a thief as he thinks." Thorn tried to clean the slime from his palms onto his pants, but without much luck.

Someone had tried to transplant light worms here, but they hadn't done too well. The section was lit by a patch barely a meter square, casting a dim light over several cell doors with a view hole at the top and a slit at the bottom.

And in front of the light was a food cart tended by a curious creature. She looked like a human girl who was about Thorn's age; but her hair had been done into alarming blue spikes with some kind of colored grease. They framed her small, slender face like a burst of rays around the sun. Around her waist was a kilt of multicolored vertical stripes, and around her neck was a breathing pearl like Thorn's.

"What tree did she drop from?" Thorn murmured to me.

She turned sharply as if she had overheard that remark. "More prisoners? I didn't bring any food for them." She looked at us in exasperation as if we had gotten ourselves thrown into the dungeon just to make more problems for her.

"You can feed them the next time." The Grand

Mage took out a ring of keys. "They're not going any place."

"Well, that won't be until tomorrow." She peevishly slid a plate underneath the slit at the base of the door.

While the Grand Mage hunted for the right key, I swam over to peer through the view hole. "Monkey, is that you?"

At the sound of my voice, a small, dirty figure, his floppy little cap askew, sat up on a bench at the back of the cell. The yellow fur was matted with dirt and blood, but the impish face was unmistakable in the pale light of the worms on the wall.

"So the Witch didn't get you after all." Monkey shuffled the two meters toward the door and stopped when he reached the end of the chains that bound him to the wall. There were patches of skin beneath the arm and leg bands as if they were too tight and had rubbed off his fur.

Monkey might have been a braggart and a fool, but he was also a survivor—and I liked that sort of person. "We fed her one of your hairs and changed it into a chain."

Monkey nodded his head with professional approval. "A bit unorthodox, but effective."

"We weren't able to change the chain back to a hair, though, so she was in pain." I flicked a claw at the Grand Mage. "But Monkey could do that. I don't know how long that sleeping potion I gave her will last."

"You seem awfully worried about her." Monkey looked at me quizzically. "From the things you told me, I thought you'd want her to suffer as much as possible."

I rested my paw against the cell door. "She was just trying to go home—like all of us."

Monkey studied me for a moment and then nodded his head grudgingly. "I think your fate and hers are intertwined somehow."

I smiled encouragingly at the Grand Mage. "So why don't you see what Monkey can do for the Witch?"

The Grand Mage adjusted his sash, which had all sorts of little pockets and loops for various magical objects. "His Exalted Majesty commanded that this thief was never to leave his cell."

Monkey started to swell out his chest but paused halfway. "I just came here for help."

"We prefer to be asked first before you take

treasures like the cauldron," the Grand Mage said icily.

"It would have taken too long." Monkey tried to adjust his cap, but his arm was stopped by some object protruding from his chest.

The Grand Mage gave a satisfied grunt as the key turned in the door to another cell. "Well, you'll have a long time to think about the effects of impatience."

Monkey dropped his paw. "Do you think this little stone box can hold the Master of the Seventy-Two Transformations?"

"It will while that needle is in you." The Grand Mage laughed with a pleased air.

I gave a start when I realized that the object was a golden needle. "Doesn't that little bit of decoration in your chest hurt?"

Like a ham actor trying to convince himself of a role, Monkey threw back his head. "Not for a master magician like Monkey. It's just . . . inconvenient."

Thorn had squeezed his head in beside me. "But what's that supposed to do?"

Monkey dropped his arm. "There's magic flowing through all of us, boy—like the currents in the sea and the ocean; and the needle breaks the connection."

"Then take it out," Thorn suggested.

Monkey shook his head with a sad little clink of his chains. "I wish I could, but if I were to do that, I'd die. It would take someone as powerful as my master, the Old Boy, to break the spell."

The Grand Mage jerked open the door to our cell. "Inside, you two. You've got the rest of your lives to discuss magic."

The cell was the same cramped size as Monkey's—about three meters on each side. Thorn thrashed his way uncertainly into the room. "Why don't the chains rust away? They're iron, aren't they?"

I squeezed into the cell after him. "Any iron in the dragon kingdom has a spell cast on it."

The Grand Mage pointed to two golden needles, each about four centimeters long, that were stuck into the sash that was wound over his shoulder. "You might want to reduce yourself," he said to me. "Once I put these needles in, you won't be able to change your size."

I tried to draw myself up; but my head bumped against the low ceiling. "I'm a princess of the royal blood; and a princess must be of the proper height."

The Grand Mage shrugged. "Suit yourself. But at normal size, this room will feel like a second hide—especially since you're going to have your pet in with you."

"I'm not a pet," Thorn corrected the Grand Mage.

But suddenly I had an idea of how to get out of here. I pretended to glance at Thorn. "I guess there wouldn't really be much room for him. And," I added, "my instructor in court etiquette said that courtesy to friends sometimes takes precedence over dignity. Very well," I said, "but you'll have to help me then. I've always used my pearl to make the change."

"Oh, very well," the Grand Mage grumbled impatiently.

I felt sharp twinges in my joints as the bones began to compact. Wincing, I passed my hand over my face, but that let me touch the spot in my forehead where the pearl was as I muttered two quick spells. And as I felt my hind legs, I moved my claws quickly in signs so that the two golden needles in the Grand Mage's sash would become invisible and two other needles would take their place. A double spell like that wouldn't last for very long, but I hoped it would work long enough.

When I had shrunk to a little over a meter, I pointed at the boy. "Is it really necessary to put the needle into the boy? He can't work any magic."

"I have my orders." The Grand Mage drew the two needles out of his sash and I held my breath, afraid that he might notice that something was wrong with them. But either the spells were stronger than I had thought or the Grand Mage was eager to get away from the cold, slimy dungeons. He breathed on the needles and, rolling them between his fingers, stuck one of them into my chest.

"You're going to regret this." Thorn stood up to the Grand Mage like the regular little soldier he was. But I was afraid his feistiness would ruin another escape plan.

"Oh, shut up." I scowled at him urgently. "Will you let me fight my own battles?"

Thorn rounded on his heel and gave me a shocked, hurt look. "I thought we were partners."

At that moment, I didn't care what I said so long as it made him keep quiet. "Sometimes this partnership doesn't work so well."

Thorn opened and closed his mouth several times as if he couldn't believe what he'd just heard; and I felt a twinge of guilt. But I forced myself to ignore that feeling. It was better to have him be angry and quiet rather than hopeful and talkative. "I followed you into a kingdom where I'm almost the only one of my own kind and suddenly you turn your back on me."

I flattened my paw against the water as if I could force all those words back into him. "Just keep your mouth shut, all right?"

Squaring his shoulders bravely, he faced the Grand Mage—as if he were expecting to be executed. "I'm ready," he announced.

But the Grand Mage had already thrust the needle into his chest and was stepping back. "It's all done," he said briskly, and stepped out into the corridor.

As one of the guards slipped into the cell and locked him into a set of chains, the Grand Mage called, "Cheer up. In ten years, His Exalted Highness may forgive your insolence and release you."

"Ten years?" Thorn was too shocked to do anything, so that he simply sank under the weight of the chains to the ooze-covered floor.

I would have liked to comfort Thorn, but I

didn't dare with the Grand Mage there. I could only sit helplessly while the guard locked the leg bands around me.

In the meantime, though, the Grand Mage watched the entire operation with a satisfied air. "Ten years would be for good behavior. Dragons are inclined to take a longer view of things than humans."

Thorn sat dazed in the slime. "B-but humans don't live as long as dragons."

When the guard had locked me into my chains, the Grand Mage shut the door on us with a heavy clank. "You might have considered that before you threatened His Most Exalted Majesty."

Though the Grand Mage and his guards eagerly retreated down the corridor, the girl stayed behind to peek through the view hole at us. "These are the two friends who were going to free you?" she asked Monkey scornfully.

Monkey's voice floated sadly in the corridor. "I thought they'd be better treated than this."

"Humph," the girl sniffed, "she doesn't look like much of a princess."

"No," I whispered, "I guess I don't."

CHAPTER SIX

Thorn's eyes widened when he saw my paw touch my forehead. "You're up to something."

"Yes," I said curtly because I was annoyed with him for nearly spoiling a second escape attempt. There were limits to my tolerance. Though he was waiting for me to say more, I just mumbled a quick spell and made a sign and the needles disappeared.

"Well," the girl said in an impressed voice.

Thorn poked at the spot where the needle had been. "You've still got your pearl."

"They took a fake one." I examined one leg band; but my leg was more likely to break than the band. It wasn't going to be so easy to get away after all. I clicked my tongue in annoyance. "You might have trusted me to take care of things. I destroyed the flame bird, didn't I?"

I waited for an apology, but he only shrugged. "It was an honest mistake. You don't always handle things so well." He tested one of the chains but it was as solid as the leg bands. "I was just doing what I thought was best."

That topped everything as far as I was concerned. "And gotten us thrown into here, you idiot." I wrapped the chains around my paws and gave them a sharp tug; but they were embedded solidly in the wall. "And now we're trapped in the dismalest place in the palace."

I suppose that Thorn was feeling just as tired with me as I was with him. "You were the one with all the big talk about your uncle; and you were the one who wanted to come here in the first place. Why blame me?"

I made myself count to ten. "Look. Let's not waste energy by arguing. We're partners—for better or for worse."

Thorn gave his chains a frustrated yank. "Well, this is definitely one of the worse times."

"You think this is bad? We'd better get out of the dungeons before Uncle Sambar discovers the pearl is a fake." And clenching my fangs, I strained at the chains; but they still wouldn't move.

"Suit yourself." He made a point of sitting down

huffily on a bench. "Lately I just seem to get criticized every time I open my mouth."

The girl screwed up her face against the little viewing hole in the door. "Just make the chains disappear like you did the needles."

I looked around the room for something I could use to pick the lock. "Those were only illusions. The most magic I know is how to change the shape and size of things."

The girl pursed her lips for a moment before she spoke. "I'm no magician, but it seems to me that the difference between locking and unlocking the iron bands is just how the tumblers of their locks are arranged. So that's just a form of shape-changing."

I looked at Thorn in amazement. "Of course. It's so simple that it was too obvious."

Thorn pulled at his chains irritably. "We would have thought of it sooner or later." I imagine that after the harsh things I had said to him, hearing me praise someone else was like another insult. The girl, though, didn't help any.

"It might have been too *late* as far as you were concerned," she declared smugly.

I tried to picture the pattern of tumblers on the

locks. They looked pretty simple so I muttered a hasty spell.

When it didn't work, the girl urged, "Don't get discouraged. Try another." She pressed her face closer to the view hole to see better, and her voice came muffled through the door. "Are you really a princess? You don't look like the others."

"I've had a slightly different sort of education." I wrinkled my forehead, trying to picture another pattern. It took two more tries before the leg and arm bands finally dropped away and let us float upward again.

The girl slammed a fist against the door triumphantly. "I knew it would work." She seemed to have taken a proprietary interest in our escape.

"Now for the door." I glided toward it eagerly.

"What's happening, Indigo?" Monkey demanded from across the way.

While the girl went to explain, I began to work on the lock to the door. It took a bit longer because the tumblers were more complicated; but I got it open after only a few tries.

When Monkey heard us swim into the corridor, he called to us softly. "Now free me."

I swam over to peer through the view hole.

Monkey seemed so hopeful and eager. "The Grand Mage only thought he was putting real needles into us. My pearl deals in illusion, not in counterspells. But I'll try." Touching the pearl, I began to mutter what I hoped was the right spell; but nothing happened.

After a dozen tries, a disappointed Monkey squatted on the slimy floor of the cell. "Then bring a flower to me. Do that and I'll help you restore your sea."

Puzzled, I stared at Monkey. "What do you want a flower for?"

Monkey clapped his paws on his knees. "I'll summon the Lord of the Flowers."

I stared at Monkey a moment, but he seemed perfectly serious. "He's the last one I'd ask for help."

Monkey rubbed the base of the needle. "He's the only one I can reach from here."

Thorn's curiosity got the better of him and he tapped my shoulder. "Who is he?"

"He's a very ancient lord," I explained, "and very whimsical. A village once asked him to end a drought and he sent rains for thirty days. The village is still a lake."

"But he can be stirred to great things," Monkey felt obliged to say.

"He's also more unpredictable than a whirlwind," I countered. "If he's your best hope, then I pity you."

Monkey tried to ease the manacle that was scraping one wrist. "Let me worry about that. Just get me the flower."

I gave a snort. "We're in the middle of an ocean. How can I find a flower? It'd be easier for me to go back to the mainland and find your master, the Old Boy."

Monkey sighed. "And only Heaven knows where in ten thousand worlds he might be."

A flap of Indigo's legs sent her up in the water like some angry hummingbird. "But there must be islands," she suggested. "And where there are islands, there must be flowers."

I studied the girl curiously because I wasn't sure why a servant girl would want to help the ape. "As far as I can recall my geography, the nearest island must be nearly three hundred kilometers away. That's a long swim—especially when I'm not my uncle's favorite relative."

Monkey rose a little shakily. "Couldn't you have

[71]

been lovable for once in your life and charmed your uncle?"

I wrinkled my nose. "Couldn't you have been humble for once and asked for help?"

Monkey picked up his plate from its spot beneath the door. "I would have wound up here even faster than I did. Your kin would have wanted my iron rod back."

I shut the door to our former cell. "As I recall, it was a magical rod that belonged to the King of the Golden Sea; and you bullied him into giving it to you."

"He wasn't using it." Monkey began to munch a mussel, shell and all.

I twisted around to look at Indigo. "The King of the Golden Sea will probably be coming for his treasure."

The girl folded her arms. "He's been sent for, but he hasn't arrived yet. In the meantime, the rod is in the vault with the cauldron and the other magical treasures. And they're protected even better than Monkey."

"Take my word for it," Monkey said with a hollow laugh. "The vault's defenses are tough."

I put my snout against the view hole. "Be patient. I'll see what I can do once we're back on the mainland."

Monkey sat down on the bench and began to slop food into his mouth. "I don't have much choice."

"That's all that you're going to do?" The girl swam forward to butt me lightly in the side. "He said you would free him."

Monkey swallowed hastily. "Indigo, you'll have to trust them as I do. They'll get me free eventually and once that happens I'll see that you reach your homeland." He used the same soothing tone you might use with a complaining kitten.

But Indigo refused to be put off. Instead, she grabbed my leg. "Take me with you. I'm almost as bad off as the prisoners here."

The last thing I needed was to be stuck with another human child. "It would be dangerous to go with us."

The girl's eyes narrowed as if I had just shoved her hard. "I know that. But I'd still prefer taking my chances with you to staying another day here."

"You must be desperate if you want to come with *us*." And while I pitied her, my conscience just wouldn't let me take her with us. "Believe me. You'll be a lot better off waiting."

It was strange to watch Indigo's face. Her eyes took on a distant, hostile look as if her soul had retreated into a fort. And her face muscles seemed to stiffen so that her mouth became fixed into a grim, hard line; and her face itself became like a fortress wall.

"I might have to wait years for another chance like this." She pressed her lips together tightly as if she were trying hard not to beg any more than she already had. "We need one another. I need a guide to the mainland; and you need someone to show you how to get out of the palace."

During my wanderings I have probably met more human liars than any dragon could possibly dream of. But she just didn't have that look. In fact, from what I'd seen of her, she seemed too impatient to bother with lying. However, I had a third rule for survival: Never take more than you can carry. "I'm sorry," I said as I gently tried to shake her loose. "You'll be far safer here."

She let go of my leg and drifted upward. "There are more important things than being safe." She raised her arm slowly and pointed her index finger at us as if she were sighting an arrow within a taut bow. "If you don't take me with you, I'll raise the alarm."

I realized then that the girl didn't care whether she lived or died. I'd certainly known that mood during all those long years away from my kind; but before I could say anything, Thorn had lunged over and grabbed her arms. "Just what kind of selfish pig are you?" He pulled her away from me.

Indigo darted a defiant glance over her shoulder. "A desperate one."

That was still no excuse for a brave, generous soul like Thorn. He looked at her contemptuously as if she had just sunk to the bottom of his list of disgusting creatures and then looked over her head at me. "Let's just tie her up and gag her."

Indigo whipped her legs so that both she and Thorn spun sideways against a wall. Startled, Thorn let go, and the girl grabbed his wrist and flung him to the floor. The next moment she was straddling his chest. "If you're going to tie me up, you'd better get some help."

Well, she had been clever enough about the locks; and she might be right about our needing help to escape from this wretched place. "All right. You can come."

Thorn looked at me as if I had just knocked him

down and sat on him myself. "You can't give in to threats from the likes of . . . of that creature."

I'd have to explain my reasons to him later when we were alone. So all I did was to snatch Indigo off of the boy before she could hit him. "I don't have time for you to beat her two falls out of three." I was sorry that I'd said that when I saw his hurt expression so I tried to give him another excuse. "Besides, she knows the palace better than I do."

"That's right." Indigo swam over to the cart and set her feet on the floor. "Now you'd better disguise yourselves. The guards don't keep track of how many servants serve the meals, but they'd be suspicious if they saw another human or a dragon your size." She jerked a thumb at Thorn. "And while you're at it, see what you can do about disguising that one's mouth."

"Don't let that sharp tongue fool you," Monkey called from his cell. "She has a good heart. It's just that it isn't easy for her in the kitchen. Her parents are dead and there's no one to protect her but herself."

"And from what I've seen, I bet you do very well," I said to her.

She couldn't help giving a smug chuckle. "Well, I've got all the other kitchen servants afraid of me."

Thorn drew himself up self-righteously as if he were once again facing Uncle Sambar. "You're going to find that we aren't so easy to bully," Thorn warned. And he gave her a scowl as big as the grimace of those guardian statues that humans place by tombs to scare away evil spirits. There wasn't going to be much love lost between the two of them.

CHAPTER SEVEN

After I had changed Thorn and myself into two elderly dragons, I wanted to swim away from the dungeons as fast as I could. A slimy cell was the last place that I wanted to stay; and Thorn felt the same way. When we had gone up to the next level, he tried to slip in front of the slow-moving food cart; but Indigo caught him by the leg as he swam overhead. "Don't be a fool. We have to take our time or the guards will be suspicious." She flicked an orange centipede from the food cart. "What's the matter? Don't you like my usual stroll through the palace?"

Thorn hurriedly paddled over a white tentacle that oozed out through the food slot of one door. "Stroll?" He stared suspiciously at her as if he were expecting some sort of trick.

However, Indigo was just being straightfor-ward. "All the other kitchen servants are grateful that I'm willing to do this, so no one bothers me." She purposefully rammed the tentacle with the cart and it shot back inside the cell. "I can take my time and think about things."

Thorn gave a shiver as he floated behind her. "I'd only get nightmares."

Indigo squinted at Thorn as if she couldn't quite believe how simple he was. "Then you've never really known what trouble was. The mind can go any place it wants—from the Spirit Gorge to the Green Darkness."

Suddenly a group of guards rounded the corner. The guard in the lead held a conch shell in his left paw while his right paw swept imperiously through the water. "Out of our way."

"Quick, obey them," Indigo grunted to us. Thorn and I hastily pressed ourselves against one wall while Indigo tried to swing her cart to the side; but apparently it wasn't fast enough for the guard who slapped her hard with the back of his paw. She hit the floor and slid a few meters over the slimy floor.

He glared down at her as she lay there. "When

I say move, I mean move, girl." With an abrupt lash of his tail, he tipped over the cart, and the dirty plates fell in slow motion.

Indigo lay sullenly on the floor, and though she held a hand to her face, I could see the bruise there. She didn't seem all that surprised by such brutal treatment—just resentful. And I could understand why she wanted to leave.

I pretended to cower against the wall as five more guards arched like boastful porpoises over the overturned cart. With them, though, was the Grand Mage. He glided over the cart, but halted. "Just a moment." He squinted hard at me as I floated in the water. "How do we know that one of these isn't the outlaw? The pearl could help her change her shape." From his sash, he removed a mage's wand—a small dagger with five ornamental blades that sprang from the hilt. I suppose he was going to work some spell that would return a shape-changer to her true form.

So my uncle had finally discovered the deception. We were too late. I tensed, deciding that it was better to die fighting than to let them take me back to a cell. From the way that Thorn was already crouching, ready to spring from a wall, I could see that he was thinking the same thing.

But right then, Indigo leapt up into the water. "Don't just stand there. Help me right this cart." And grabbing one of my ankles, she began to slap me. The blows didn't hurt me through my thick hide, but they did startle me. At first, I was going to bend downward and hit back—when I saw her wink. Suddenly I began to suspect what the quick-witted girl was up to; and it was all right. After all, I had put up with worse humiliations during my wanderings among humans. But I was now glad that I'd taken her along.

However, when she grabbed hold of Thorn and struck him, he balled his paws up as if they were fists. "What—?" Thorn began to object; but I gestured for him to keep quiet. And for once he saw and understood.

"Yes, yes." Righting the cart, I dropped to the floor and motioned him down beside me. Together Thorn and I bent quickly to help Indigo pick up the scattered plates.

"Come on," the guard urged the Grand Mage. "Do you think a princess of the royal blood would let a servant beat her? She's still got that pin you stuck into her. She can't work magic."

The Grand Mage patted his sash as if he weren't all that sure. "I suppose so."

"Then let's hurry," the guard called. His voice drifted down the corridor as if he had already gone along several strokes.

The Grand Mage hesitated a moment, and Indigo added an undignified kick to my rump. "The cook's going to make you pay for your clumsiness when we get to the kitchen."

I let my voice rise in a high, complaining whine. "But the guard knocked it over."

"He did it because the cart didn't move fast enough." Indigo paddled overhead menacingly. "You should have been helping me."

"As you say." I tried to put all the resignation that I could into my voice.

The Grand Mage snorted contemptuously. "No, where there's no spirit, there's no princess." With a swirl of his tail, he whirled around and hurried after the guards.

As soon as he was out of sight, Indigo righted the cart and then dropped to her knees to help me gather the rest of the plates and put them onto the cart. "I hope you don't mind," she whispered to me.

"Mind?" I gave a chortle. "I thought it was brilliant, child. Simply brilliant."

It still seemed as if I couldn't say anything good about Indigo without hurting Thorn. "What's so smart about it?" he demanded. "She should have just beaten me."

I wiped my paws on a wall because they were slimy from the floor. "It wouldn't have convinced them."

He rose indignantly. "I see. Insults count for more down here than bravery."

"Let's save this chat for some other occasion, shall we? I think we'd better run now." Indigo began to trundle the cart up the corridor and Thorn and I added our strength to it. We hurried up several levels until we were finally rumbling toward the stone door that separated the dungeons from the palace.

The guard there was a dragon with wide haunches. He only bothered to look at Indigo as we rushed up. I guess it was as she had said—the dungeon guards were too sleepy to count the number of servants. "What's happening?"

"I don't know," Indigo said breathlessly, "but the guards were in an awful hurry."

"So are you," the guard laughed as he shot the bolt back on the door.

"I should be able to exchange this bit of gossip for some treat from the cooks." Indigo danced from one foot to the other in her impatience.

"Well, give me some on your next trip," the guard laughed, and waved us on through.

She guided the cart for about four hundred meters down one corridor before she tried to lead it up another.

Thorn immediately dragged it to a halt. "It seems like you're taking us right into the middle of the palace," Thorn said suspiciously. "But we'll need an exit that most people won't use."

"I know that. But first I want to get some food for us. Or are you going to filter the plankton with those big teeth of yours?" She yanked the cart disgustedly out of our grasp. "I've been waiting for years to meet another human being. I can't say that I'm very impressed. They aren't all fools like you, are they?"

Thorn waved her away irritably. "So why don't you just stay here?"

Her eyelids had lowered, giving her an angry yet distant look—as if she were hiding somewhere inside herself. "I want to go home. It'll be different there." With a jerk of her head for us to follow, she began to shove the cart forward.

I used to talk about my home in just the same way. It made me realize that it couldn't have been any easier for a human child isolated among dragons than it had been for me among humans. In her own way, she was a kindred soul, and that made me raise a paw to still Thorn. "And where's home?"

The cart began to rattle as she pushed it even harder. "The Green Darkness."

The Green Darkness was the name given to a very ancient forest on the coast; and it took me a moment before I remembered the name of its inhabitants. "The Kingfisher clan lives there, doesn't it?"

She regarded me suspiciously—torn for a moment between not wanting to expose herself more, and her own natural curiosity about her home. "Yes, my father was the head of the clan; and when he objected to some of the Butcher's plans for our people, my parents had to flee to the palace. But they're both dead now."

It wasn't usual for dragons to grant asylum to

humans even when they were escaping someone as vicious as the Butcher. But the Kingfisher clan were a folk whose simple ways went back to the early days of the world; and there had been many dragon friends among them. Of course, humans live such short lives compared to dragons that it's easy to lose track of them; but perhaps one of Indigo's ancestors had been just such a dragon friend.

I caught a plate before it fell off. "They must have missed the Green Darkness terribly. It's a lovely place."

She forgot to be defensive in her sudden excitement. "You've been there?"

"In my wanderings, yes." We swung the cart onto a level corridor. "Let's see. It would have been some hundred years ago; but I remember the old trees."

Indigo raised one hand slowly as if she were caressing the trunk of one of them. "My mother said that they went back to the very creation of the world."

"They looked tall enough for it." Sadly, I remembered how I had once been just as enthusiastic about seeing my home until I'd found it a wasteland. "They're certainly the last survivors of the old forests. I've heard it said that they once covered all the land."

It was a pleasure to see Indigo perk up. "And did you have some of the honey?"

"It was some of the best honey I ever had." I pressed a claw against my snout for a moment while I tried to remember. "But as I recall the special dish was a kind of berry cake."

Indigo's mouth suddenly cracked into a smile, and it was like seeing the gates open in a dark fortress, letting out a flood of light. "Made with special almonds that grow only on the peninsula." She added enthusiastically, "And there was a stew made with trout and crayfish."

Actually I didn't remember what fish it was, but I found myself wanting to protect her. After all, I'd just had my own dreams of a grand welcome rudely shattered. So I lied. "Yes, that too."

"All that talk is making me hungry." Indigo let go of the cart so that it rolled into a storage room. "Stay here and I'll be back with supplies." And she swam off before either of us could stop her.

Thorn shifted uneasily, and the motion made him rise in the water. "Are you going to take her word? She might be going to turn us in. Maybe they'd give her a reward and a free trip to the Green Darkness."

I nudged him inside. "She could have told the Grand Mage who we were."

Thorn floated in the water with his head pulled back toward his shoulders and his paws up like some boxer getting ready for a fight. "I still don't see why you gave in to blackmail."

I thought for a moment about my conversation with Indigo on the way here. "She's not as tough as she pretends to be—like the hard shell around a nut that protects the tenderness inside. Only her tenderness isn't food; it's a dream."

Thorn clenched and unclenched his paws. "About going to the Green Darkness?"

I curled my tail about a giant jar to hold myself in place. "I think she's survived by holding onto a dream—and keeping herself worthy of that dream."

From the look on his face, you would have thought that I had just helped her kick him. "I've been through a lot for you; and she's only threatened you—and yet you keep taking her side."

I gave his leg a good-natured poke. "It's only

been a couple of times. Don't be jealous."

He snapped his leg back sharply as if I had just contaminated it. "It's just that I only seem to do everything wrong and she seems to do everything right."

Finally, I understood. "If I hurt your feelings before, I'm sorry," I said as gently and reassuringly as I could. "But we were in dangerous situations when I didn't have the time to make polite apologies."

He gripped a shelf and drew himself toward the floor. "I've been scared ever since we entered the sea; but I've tried to do my best."

I pursed my lips together and nodded my head encouragingly. "It takes a brave heart to challenge the High King and to go into the dungeons without complaining."

He shot a hard glance at me. "But I just seem to irritate you."

I drew my teeth along my upper lip while I sought the right words. "Well, it would help if you were a bit more . . . um . . . flexible."

But he was still so hurt and so intent on feeling sorry for himself that he twisted my words. I might just as well have been trying to bridge a canyon with only threads. "Maybe you've found someone better—like Indigo."

I was some fine princess who couldn't even hold onto a court made up of one person. "I think we still have a long road to travel together."

Unconvinced, he curled up on his side as if he were trying to pull himself into a protective little ball. "Perhaps we ought to discuss this once we're safely on land; but I'm beginning to think that you're right: This partnership doesn't always work."

I felt so helpless right then. I knew how to outfight and outswim and outfly most anyone; but I didn't know how to regain that closeness we'd had when we'd first entered the dragon kingdoms.

I was still hunting for something to say when a panting Indigo returned a little while later. In her hands was a sack of food and bulbs of fresh water as well as two kitchen knives. "Come on. Let's go."

Thorn craned his neck up so he could see over her head and almost seemed disappointed that there wasn't a horde of warriors trailing behind her. And as we swam down the corridor, he kept looking behind him as if he expected them to spring out at any moment.

Finally, Indigo looked back at him. "What's the matter?"

"A variety of nastinesses that aren't there," I quipped. "But don't you have anything you want to take with you besides that?" I pointed at the sack of food.

She gave a hitch to the sack. "I don't have anything. My parents died when I was small and the other servants took away everything they owned."

Suddenly the sound of someone blowing a conch shell echoed down the corridor. Indigo, who was in the lead, stopped swimming abruptly. "What's that?"

But I knew that sound from maneuvers in the Inland Sea. "It must be the imperial guard." I grimaced. "I'm afraid that they know we're on the loose." I leaned my head to the side to try to hear better. "But it sounds like they're ordering a systematic search level by level."

Indigo whipped her legs together suddenly so that she shot forward. "We'd better hurry, then."

"But we're in disguise and you work here," Thorn protested.

"They'll be taking in everyone for interrogation. And the mages will be able to change us back to our true shapes," I explained, and darted past Thorn. "So I, for one, don't intend to wait around."

"Me neither." Flailing his legs awkwardly, Thorn drew level with me. "I've already stayed longer than I wanted to in that dungeon."

CHAPTER EIGHT

Indigo didn't hesitate as she led us down winding corridors into a dimly lit section of the palace in which I had never been before. Despite the problems with Thorn, I was beginning to think that I had been right to take her along.

Eventually, she led us into a large, oval-shaped room nearly a quarter of a kilometer broad. Mirrors had been inset into the curving floor and walls. As Thorn paused in the water, dozens of him seemed to drift all around us in the distance. "What is this place?" Thorn wondered.

"A ballroom." I pointed to a large balcony hanging from the ceiling. "The orchestra would be there. But," I added, "I don't think this particular room has been used in a long time." Some mage had cast his or her magic well, for barnacles and coral worms still did not mar the surface of the mirrors. But the orchestra balcony must not have been covered by such spells. Sea creatures clustered so thickly on it that it was impossible to tell its original shape.

The ballroom itself ended at huge windows formed from polished shells each about the size of my head. They were set into a framework of some light metal; but many of the panes were broken now and fish swam in and out of the holes.

Indigo kicked her way over toward one hole. "They haven't used this room in ages—not since your uncle's father built the new ballroom, or so I've heard."

She paused beside one of the huge windows and worked at a latch. Behind us, we could hear a conch shell blow from our left in the distance. Another shell answered it from our right.

"That's the guard." I shoved Thorn toward Indigo. Indigo began to struggle with the window. "Help me with this."

I swam over with Thorn. The magic that had originally protected the metal must have been wearing thin because the latch had begun to fuse itself to the frame, and small, acorn-shaped mussels had begun to grow on the edges of the frame itself.

The conch shells sounded closer. I began to use my claws to scrape at the mussels so that they went tumbling through the water.

Though their words weren't distinct, we could hear the guards' bored tones—as if this search were only part of a routine. I shoved Indigo's paw away and closed my own around the latch. The metal screeched in protest as I twisted it, and the sound seemed to echo through the ballroom. A moment later, the conch shell began to blow a series of urgent notes.

"That's done it." Thorn frantically began to try the windows to our right.

I wrenched at the latch and felt it come off in my hand. I stared at the twisted metal dumbly for a moment and then pitched it away. I heard it crack a mirror beneath us. "There's only one thing to do." I waved Indigo away from me. "Watch out."

I arched backward through the water in a large loop so that I was some ten meters from the window. Both Indigo and Thorn were at a safe distance. With a kick of my legs and a twist of my tail, I shot toward the window. The panes seemed to rush toward me like a web of frosted light; but just before I was about to smash into it, I swirled around in the water and brought my heavy tail around. The metal frame screamed and panes of shell broke with merry tinklings under the blow.

In the corridor, the guards were shouting excitedly to one another now. I looked through the hole. The open sea seemed so inviting; but I knew an inexperienced swimmer like Thorn could never outswim the guards. Still, the other choice was almost as dangerous because I didn't know if I had enough time to work that much magic.

As Indigo and Thorn churned their way up to me, I held up a paw. "Hold still, you two." Touching my forehead, I worked a quick sign and saw Thorn begin to shrink, his head and snout fusing into his shoulders while his scales turned to silver. I didn't wait to see if he had finished changing into a brother to one of the fish that swam in the ballroom. Instead, I faced Indigo and quickly cast a spell on her. Her body began to shorten as well, the sack becoming a brown bump near her spine.

The guards were very close to the door now. I

touched my forehead. "Please," I begged the pearl, "help me quickly." And I felt the pearl tingle as it had in the audience room—almost as if it were having immense fun now.

My head snapped down hard on my neck and I felt the bones jam together as I began to shrink.

"The noise came from in here," one guard said from the corridor.

I turned, but no one was in the doorway yet. I felt lighter and sleeker in the water and I could feel my eyelids peeling back as they became the unblinking eyes of a fish.

A conch shell blew loudly as three guards swam into the ballroom. One of them was the same officious lieutenant who had escorted us to the palace. "There." He pointed to the broken window. "They must have gone out this way." He darted through the water toward the opening.

One of the guards raised a conch shell to his lips; and his chest and cheeks expanded and collapsed like a blowfish. From all around the palace, conch shells answered him. The other guard, however, stayed in the doorway, her eyes alertly studying the fish that swam around the abandoned ballroom. "Sir," she inquired in a polite but firm voice, "shouldn't we wait for a mage to help with any disguises?"

"And lose time chasing them?" The lieutenant waved an impatient paw. "Hurry ub. They can't have gone far." I think he already had visions of further promotions once we were captured.

"I could have sworn I saw one of these fish change from green to silver when we came into the room." Her eyes momentarily fixed on me; and it was the hardest thing not to rush out through the window. But instead, I made myself take my eyes away from her and curve in a leisurely circle. Just keep swimming, I told myself. Just keep swimming.

"It was only a trick of the light," the lieutenant insisted. "Now if you want to stay in the guard, you'll come with me."

I could have kissed the lieutenant for his stubbornness—thank Heaven that you can count on some people to be so consistently stupid. But, of course, I did nothing that would have tipped off my identity. Instead, I concentrated on swimming in a casual manner as the guard reluctantly kicked her way toward the window.

"Come along, you fool." The lieutenant swatted

the guard with his tail. She snapped her teeth as if there were nothing she would have liked better than to have taken a bite out of the lieutenant; but she was disciplined enough to swim through the window. Thank Heaven too, that guards are taught to obey orders even from fools like the lieutenant.

The lieutenant gestured a paw as grandly as any general—which he might have been already in his own imagination. "Send the others after us," he instructed the conch blower, and then swam after the sullen guard.

I picked out Indigo by the brown spot on her back. Near her was a fish that I thought was Thorn. I jerked my head surreptitiously at them to follow me toward the window. I didn't intend to wait here while a horde of the imperial guard thrashed through the ballroom. There was too much of a chance that one of them might grab one of us for a quick snack.

I wriggled in a straight line toward the window but did a small, quick loop to look behind me and make sure that the two fish were squirming after me. Reassured, I darted through the window and into the open waters above the gardens.

The gardens must have been nice at one time,

but this particular section had been neglected along with the ballroom. I could see a few antique statues lying like corpses among the coral and sea anemones. A kind of corrugated coral was growing over the pedestals so that it looked as if they were acquiring red-colored skins.

The lieutenant and the alert guard were two distant dots already as he charged after phantoms. I swam low, down among the coral, and Thorn and Indigo copied me. With conch shells blowing, two dozen of the guard came boiling through the window—so many in fact that the frame shattered, scattering panes of shell like giant flower petals over the garden. They moved in such a dense, tightly packed column that they looked like they were fused into one giant centipede's body.

"Wait," I murmured to the others as I watched the dragons thrash on past. Both Indigo and Thorn pressed close against me as if for reassurance. I could feel the small wrigglings of their bodies against mine and I remembered that, for all their bold talk, they were only humans, after all.

When the dragons were gone, I whispered to them. "We're going to have to swim very low— down at two hundred meters where it's dark—so stay close to me. They'll be expecting us to head west to the mainland, so we'll go east."

"But," Indigo protested as quietly as she could, "that's where the Abyss is and we've been having troubles with kraken raiders lately."

So apparently the humans weren't the only ones who were getting bolder. "We won't be going as far as the Abyss." I wriggled a fin in that direction. "We'll travel only as far as the Spine." The Spine was the name given to the great ridge of undersea mountains and volcanoes that ran down the middle of the ocean. "Then we'll turn north and travel a good distance before we head west. Maybe we can slip around my uncle's troops that way."

I began to swim through the coral. It had grown so wild that what had once been neat, orderly arrangements of coral and anemones were now as wild a tangle as any sea reef; but that gave us plenty of hiding places. Overhead, we could hear more conch shells blowing as more of the guard joined the pursuit.

Eventually, though, the garden had to thin out as the ridge began to drop into the darkness. "Are you ready?" I asked the other two. The shadows made it hard to see them, but I thought that they nodded their heads. "Don't be scared of the dark. Darkness never hurt anyone," I said and added to myself, It's just the things that might hide in the darkness that could be dangerous.

CHAPTER NINE

With a flip of my tail, I rose from the coral. The closest dragons looked like hen tracks scratched on the surface of the sea. Since my head and body were fused together as a unit, I had to lower my whole torso to see that Thorn and Indigo were poking their faces cautiously from the coral. Jerking my body for them to follow me, I started to swim down the slope.

At a hundred meters, all the colors of the rocks began to fade into one brownish-gray shade, and at a hundred and fifty meters, even the outlines of the rocks began to blur. We were at the point in the sea where the sunlight had never reached and never would. I felt as small as an ant and even the mountains didn't seem any larger than mounds of dirt piled on a tray of black lacquer.

We swam slowly over the edge of visible light; but I felt less like I was swimming and more like I was flying—like some bird that had soared so high it had flown above the night sky.

Indigo drew so close to me that her trembling side pressed against me. If she had ever been away from the palace, I don't think it had been at night-time. Gone was all the assurance she had shown in the palace maze. Now she was only another small, helpless creature. "It's all right," I tried to reassure her. "The plankton will rise soon."

It was the wrong thing to say.

"I'm not scared." Indigo drew away but I could still feel how her quivering body made the water move.

With a flick of my tail, I turned sideways so that I could see her with both my eyes. "Then you're braver than I was when I was first expelled. I thought it was weakness to depend on anyone."

She opened and closed her mouth several times; but it was hard to tell whether it was a reflex of her fish's body or because she was searching for something to say. Finally, she just gave an angry lash of her tail. "So, good for you." And she darted ahead of us.

"Charming company, isn't she?" Thorn muttered to me.

I strained my eyes to see her, but she was already only a dot. It was strange, but I had the feeling that I had just looked into a mirror. "She reminds me of myself at a certain age."

Thorn had to move his entire fish body up and down in a nod as if he were finally beginning to understand. "But she isn't a human version of you."

"Maybe. Maybe not." I started to paddle after her. "But I'd at least like to convince her that she doesn't have to do it all by herself." I swam a little faster; but she had stopped when she realized she was losing sight of us.

"Is this the way?" she asked irritably—as if she needed a reason to rejoin us.

Not only had I lost my one friend, but I couldn't even help this younger self learn from my mistakes. It seemed that I was a failure at being a dragon as well as at being a princess. "Yes," I sighed. "We seemed to have reached one of the deep ocean currents that flows eastward. We can settle into it and let it do most of the work." When Thorn joined us, I drifted a little higher. Though I couldn't see them, I could feel the motions their bodies made in the water. "We'll take turns sleeping. One of us will keep watch to make sure the other two don't drift too far away. I'll take the first watch."

As frightening as the sea might be, it had been a long, straining day, and first Thorn and then Indigo dropped off to sleep. Their bodies slowed from steady, rhythmic movements to an occasional sluggish twitch as their sleeping bodies instinctively made a motion to keep them at the same level.

As a result, I was the only one who was awake when tiny, glowing shrimp rose about us. They seemed to rise like a cloud of stars that someone had flung up toward us—drifting upward in slow motion. It was almost as if we were back at the creation of the universe. I could feel the other two near me, but not see them. And the stars were soaring toward us, expanding to fill the sea.

And then I thought I saw something near the top of the rising cloud of shrimp—a sleek, white shape. I dropped lower, but it seemed to have disappeared. I thought to myself, perhaps it's just a large fish; but the white shape appeared again. The shovel-like form was unmistakable. It was a kraken; but I couldn't understand what it was doing so deep in the dragon kingdoms, for we were still far away from the Abyss.

I let myself drift upward, and I gave a gentle bump first to Thorn and then to Indigo. "Be still," I whispered, and we stopped in the water—though the current itself kept tugging us along. I had hoped that the kraken wouldn't notice us; but nothing much escaped its greedy senses. It was said that krakens could smell a dragon a kilometer away and hear one at two.

It began to rise in a conelike spiral toward us. And even as I watched, two more followed it out of the darkness below. The dim, eerie plankton lit their bodies just enough so I could make out the blunt, shovel-like heads. Two small eyes grew on either side of each head just before they ended in bony, collar-like shields. A row of mean looking spikes marched down each spine.

We couldn't outswim them and in my present shape I couldn't outfight them. We would have to change back. I wriggled one fin in an awkward sign and murmured the spell. This time I felt as if my bones were stretching faster than my skin. It didn't hurt so much as it itched terribly.

Even though the fin on my right side had not quite changed into a claw, I held it out. "Quick, get on my paw."

An alarmed Thorn swam past my snout into my paw. "What are those things?"

I clenched my left forepaw and then unclenched it. My claws were almost ready. "Krakens. They like to boast that they don't even leave one small fish alive after their raids."

Indigo reluctantly rested on my right forepaw beside Thorn. "I tried to warn you. They've been raiding further and further from the Abyss for a long time now."

"And I should have listened." I closed my right forepaw around their fragile bodies and whirled around. My hind legs had not quite formed and my scales still had a soft, silvery glow; but the krakens were not about to let me finish changing. I slashed with my left forepaw at the lead kraken and he sheered off, momentarily exposing the soft flesh between his bony collar and the first of the spikes along his spine.

With a back-wrenching lash of my body, I shot toward that vulnerable spot and sank my fangs in. At the very same instant, I spread my half-formed wings despite the sudden pain I felt at making changing bones do their work too soon; but the extra drag of the wings was just enough to make us jerk to a halt in the water. And for a moment the kraken floated there in confusion. That was all the time I needed to finish it off.

As the corpse began to drop back into the darkness, the spiked bodies of its two companions slid upward past me. I saw the leathery undersides of their heads with the pouting slits fringed with needlelike teeth as they passed. They looked more like exotic flowers than mouths; but I knew that once those mouths fastened on a victim, they didn't let go until they had drained every drop of blood.

As the krakens halted ten meters above me, I turned, trying to keep my right forepaw with Thorn and Indigo away from them; but the deadly creatures merely swam in a slow, tight circle. When I feinted an attack, they simply rose a meter higher; but when I tried to drop lower, they followed.

I began to swim along in the current. "They don't want us to get to the surface and fly away."

Indigo squirmed in my right forepaw and I relaxed my grasp a little. "They'll have to leave when the sun rises."

"Why's that?" Thorn wondered.

"It's always dark in the Abyss," I explained, "so they can tolerate sunlight for only a little while."

"Well, what are they waiting for?" Thorn eyed them nervously. "Are they scared of you?"

"Krakens are more careful than cowardly." I had been dividing my attention between the krakens above us and the sea below. Finally I saw three more shovel-like shapes slip upward. "There, they were waiting for the rest of their raiding party." There was no way I was going to escape—but the two children might. I lowered my right forepaw until it was against my chest. "When I let go of you two, I want you to swim for the surface. I'll join you there and change you back to your regular shapes."

"And then?" Indigo demanded.

"Then we'll fly somewhere," I lied.

"But won't the guard have aerial patrols?" Thorn objected.

"At the moment," I said drily, "I think I'd prefer their company to the krakens."

With a kick, I darted upwards toward the krakens; but they refused to fight. Instead, they kept swimming higher and higher until I could feel my own body tiring. And in the meantime, the other three krakens, perhaps because they were fresher, were gaining on us. They would catch up with me long before we reached the surface; and by that time I would be worn out.

I had only one real choice then: to fight at lower odds and perhaps draw the two from above. In the confusion, I might be able to make my escape after all. I gave a few half-hearted kicks as if I were more tired than I actually felt. The three krakens were now only some twenty meters below me.

With a sudden arch of my back, I flung Indigo and Thorn away and looped through the water. Screaming my clan's war cry, I dove toward the three krakens. But they arched away each in a different direction. This wasn't the first time they had fought a desperate dragon.

I had an anxious moment when I wondered if I had done the right thing to drive Indigo and Thorn away. At the very least, I had hoped that I would distract the krakens enough to let them allow two fish to escape; but one could never be certain what the krakens would do. They sometimes killed simply for the joy of killing.

But I counted five krakens overhead, circling

now in a tight, deadly ring above; and even as I flexed my claws nervously, they began to dive toward me one after the other. Their heads sliced through the water and they hissed loudly so that all I could think of was arrows in flight.

I slashed at the first, though he was a white blur, and then he was gone. The next moment something battered into me like a small boulder; but as I went tumbling through the water, I knew it was only a kraken that had rammed me at full force. And even as I straightened out, I could feel a searing, fiery pain in one wing as a kraken twisted by, its spines cutting at me.

I whirled around with a snarl and gave a pained grunt as the next kraken darted by, slashing its spikes at my other wing. These krakens had had a good deal of practice disabling a dragon. Even if I got to the surface now, I couldn't fly. And since the night had only begun, I had hours till sunrise. Suddenly I knew that I was going to die.

And that certainty only filled me with a cool sort of anger. I didn't make the mistake of turning around to try to catch an attacker that was already past. Instead, I flailed my paws out blindly. I felt a fiery pain across my right forepaw, but I forced the claws to clench—though the pain only increased. I was determined to take at least one more kraken with me when I died.

The kraken thrashed in the water, trying to escape my grip by making the spike cut up my paw. But I kept a tight hold as I wrapped my other legs around it and began to use my claws and fangs on it.

The other krakens, of course, hadn't been idle. They had been busy climbing back up after their dive. I could see a kraken rising toward me, and I craned my neck around to try and bite it; but my fangs slid off the hard, tough hide stretched over its skull. And then its head was arching in. I fully expected to feel its fangs sink into my neck the next moment when something silvery streaked by my head.

Suddenly, I heard a slapping sound, and the kraken hung there startled for a moment. A second silvery shape flashed on by, circling round the heavy kraken head, and I saw the fish's needlelike teeth snapping at the left eye of the kraken. It raised its head away instinctively, and I let go of the dying kraken to attack the next one.

It was my fangs that sank through its tough hide

into its neck and it was my claws that raked its underbelly. I lifted my snout long enough to snarl at Thorn and Indigo, "I thought I told you two to get to the surface."

"We did, but you didn't seem to be doing too well so we came back." Thorn flipped over on his side away from the slashing teeth of a kraken.

I could feel fangs in my legs and my left foreleg as the remaining krakens attacked. Thorn and Indigo darted in to bite at their eyes and the confused krakens broke off, arching above us again.

My legs now felt stiff and heavy. "Thank you," I said to the two humans. "But it's only a matter of time now. Save yourselves."

Thorn's gills widened, showing the red flesh underneath his silver scales. Then he blew out a mouthful of water. "No. For better or worse, we're a team. We fight together; and if we have to, we die together."

I looked at Thorn gratefully. Apparently, he was willing to forget about past wrongs. "I won't hold you to this. After all, you're the one who wanted to talk about breaking up the team."

Thorn flicked a side fin as if he were tossing that whole argument away. "I guess I finally understand what you saw in her—I think you were wrong, by the way. But that discussion can still wait until we're both on the mainland,"

Indigo simply stared at us—and the large, open eyes of her fish shape only added force to that stare. "You won't live if you stay. You're a fool. Both of you are."

I drifted in the water, watching as the krakens circled, building up speed for their next attack. I wasn't in any mood to pamper her now. "Yes," I said drily. "I've often thought of how convenient it would have been if one of us had been smarter."

Indigo clumsily wriggled forward a meter—as if her own body were fighting her. "Well, I'm going."

Thorn had taken up a position by my right fore-paw as if he suspected that the krakens would attack on what was now my weaker side. "Fine, we'll buy time for you."

But Indigo had remained in the exact same spot. "There aren't any ties between us."

I wrinkled my brow. It seemed to me as if she were arguing more with herself than with us. And that was a good sign. It was just a shame that we probably weren't going to get to develop that impulse. "Did we say anything about ties?"

"I'm not a coward. I came back once." She squirmed in the water—which I guess was the closest a fish could come to a shrug. "But I'm no fool either."

"Indigo, you can't always be thinking of yourself." Thorn flapped his body as if experimenting with that as a weapon.

"If I don't," she countered, "who will?"

"People who only think of themselves become a race of one." I swung up my claws once again though my legs now felt as if they were simply metal tubes. When the girl didn't reply, I looked in her direction and saw that she was already darting away. I exhaled a large mouthful of water. "I hope she finds what she's looking for."

"You tried to help her." Thorn could be far more gracious than I when he was right.

The krakens had begun to peel off in their dives once again—one after the other. I glanced at him for what was probably the last time. "It would have been better for you if you'd been more like her."

Thorn flicked his tail lightly. "But I don't want to be."

"It's selfish of me, I guess; but I'm glad." As the krakens plunged downward, I raised my head and swelled my chest, getting ready to give the war cry of my clan one last time, when I suddenly heard someone yell it from far away.

CHAPTER TEN

At the first cry, the krakens had darted off to the side away from me with angry looks—as if I had caught *them* in some kind of trap. Then, as the cries grew louder, the krakens picked up speed and dove into the sheltering darkness.

Dragons plummeted past us so fast that I couldn't count all of them. Suddenly a light flared into life some twenty meters below. One of the dragons must have ripped the cover from a torch and the chemicals had ignited with the water. I could count a dozen dragons dropping like daggers through the water after the fleeing krakens.

Thorn wriggled by my snout urgently. "We should escape. Change yourself into something."

"They gave the war cry of our clan, though." I waved him away from my face.

An embarrassed Indigo wriggled back now that it was safe. "More than likely they *are* from your clan. The common folk get the dirtiest and most dangerous jobs—like fighting the krakens."

I stared into the darkness after the tiny sun that marked the dragons now. The sun whirled and darted as if there were a tremendous battle going on below. "I haven't even thought about the rest of my clan since we got here." I wagged my head guiltily from side to side. "My poor, poor people."

Indigo watched the battle below. "The question is: What will they think of you now?"

She had a point. No more daydreams of grand welcomes for me. From now on, I was going to be a hard-snouted realist. "I'm not sure how loyal I'd be after all these years of neglect." I motioned for them to go on. "Maybe you'd better go off a little way until I'm sure."

"Too late." Thorn said. "They're coming."

The dragons, fresh from their victory over the krakens, rose up all around us like deadly flowers suddenly sprouting up from black soil. These weren't the toy soldiers of the palace with their gold-tipped claws and plumed helmets, but fighters. Some looked like grizzled veterans hundreds of years old while others seemed to be newly hatched—and yet all of them bore some kind of scars.

One of them, wearing the disk with the triangular mark of a sergeant, swam forward. "I know that face." She fumbled in the pouch slung over one shoulder and took out a torch of reeds. Holding it in front of her carefully, she ripped off the covering. It flared instantly into life and I blinked my eyes against the sudden bright light.

I brought my good paw up to shield my eyes. "Have a care. I'm not some mummy in a mausoleum that you're staring at."

The sergeant pulled back the torch slightly. I couldn't help noticing that she was missing one steel-tipped claw. "And that tone."

A dragon with just a stump for one wing drifted up beside the sergeant. "I'd swear that it's the princess. So the news was true after all."

The sergeant craned her neck to the side as if she needed to study me from another angle. "We would have sworn that you were dead, though."

"It would take more than a continent of humans to do me in." I lowered my paw.

The sergeant took in the scars on my legs and

body approvingly. "And now you've fought your way back to your people, Your Highness."

The one-winged dragon glared at me resentfully. "Highness? She's no more a princess than any of us. We outlawed her ourselves."

The sergeant pulled at his tail angrily. "That was a long time ago, Slug."

Slug jerked his head at me over his shoulder. "I still don't see why I have to bow to the likes of her. She probably just came looking for a handout and when the High King told her off, she got mad and probably insulted him. That's why we've got orders to bring her back. What's her quarrel mean to us?"

I looked around at the quiet, guarded faces. "That's true. My uncle Sambar will be pleased when you return me to him."

The sergeant hissed as she drew in a mouthful of water. "If anyone's earned the right to be a princess, you have." She added pointedly, "Your Highness."

It took me a moment to find my voice. "No, Slug's right. I'm not worth much as a princess."

Slug twisted one side of his mouth up sardonically. "Well, we're not worth much as a people."

I remembered some of the things that Indigo had just said. "Your lives haven't been easy, have they?"

Slug gave a bitter laugh. "The only way to leave the garrison is to die."

The sergeant swung her head back up proudly. "But there's still a good deal of fight left in us, Your Highness."

I didn't know whether to weep or smash something and pretend it was my uncle's head. So this is what he had done to my once proud clan. "Didn't my brother fight for your rights?"

"That one." The sergeant swatted at a lilylike snail fluttering in the water as if she wished it were my brother's skull instead. "As long as the High King fed him, he didn't care what happened to the rest of us. And as soon as things got a little rough, he ran away."

Over the centuries I had thought of many sorts of punishments for my brother, Pomfret; but none of them would have been as harsh on him as a penniless exile. "Things came too easily for Pomfret. He was the eldest, after all."

"I think things came too easily for all of you," grumbled Slug.

The sergeant slid through the water as smoothly

and quietly as a knife and hooked a foreleg around Slug's neck. "For once in your life, will you use your eyes first instead of your tongue? Look at her. She's got as many scars as any of us. If anything, she's had an exile harder than any of us. At least we've always had our own kind around us."

Slug's eyes took in the marks on my body and then he dropped his head almost guiltily. "I'm sorry."

I suppose it would seem strange to you that I had never thought about what it meant to be a child of the royal blood. Everyone had been concentrating on training my older brother to rule the Inland Sea. As a result, being a princess had seemed to be a series of banquets and pageants and making appearances at whatever charitable event was happening that day.

"No," I said huskily. "No, when I was in the Inland Sea, I didn't think of much more than myself. I was probably just the sort of person you resented, Slug." I owed at least a confession to all these long-suffering folk.

The sergeant glared at Slug, who shrank back. "Well, now, you weren't much more than a child when you were expelled."

I beckoned Thorn and Indigo in close to me as

I saw several of the dragons eyeing them hungrily. "But I wonder if I would have become any better."

The sergeant patted my shoulder clumsily. "Would any of us before that cursed Witch stole our sea?"

However, Thorn hadn't learned anything about keeping his mouth shut. He gave an excited wriggle in front of my snout. "But you don't have to worry about her anymore," Thorn piped up. "The princess has captured Civet."

I caught his tail in my paw and pulled him back. "What are you doing?" I whispered to him fiercely.

But he only looked at me defiantly—as if he were determined to help me whether I liked it or not. "They ought to know what you've done for them."

"But her capture doesn't do much good while both the humans and the other dragons are angry at us," I pointed out, but it was already too late.

Surprised, the sergeant had just let herself sink in the water. Other dragons were making shrill yelps and giving short, squat kicks so that they stirred up clouds of bubbles. And the loudest and most enthusiastic yelper was Slug. "It's over, it's over. The Exile is over." And he did an excited back flip.

Suddenly the sergeant began to kick out her paws and stomp them against an invisible floor. And the others of her squad began to copy her, though they were much too close to one another. There would be a few bruises tomorrow from all the contact.

The sergeant danced around us jubilantly. "The ocean dragons laugh at us when we celebrate. They call this our drunken jellyfish dance."

A one-eyed dragon swirled on by. "But there isn't one of those ocean dragons who's fit enough to dance with us."

Slug crowed from overhead, "We can do anything better than those fat worms."

The sergeant curved her back so that she was looking at me upside down. "If you want to know the truth, they're just scared of us. All things being equal, they know we'd beat them." And she winked at me smugly.

Even Thorn squirmed out of my grasp and darted in a dizzying, silvery circle over my head. Only Indigo watched me with calm, ironic eyes—as if to ask me what I was going to do now.

"Please, please," I said to them; but it was still several moments before the sergeant could calm them long enough to listen to me; and she had the hardest time with Slug. When he finally was willing to shut up and look at me, I saw that the doubt and hostility was gone from even his face now, and instead I saw only a strange, uncomfortable kind of worship that I had never seen directed toward me.

"I'm still a fugitive from the High King's justice," I cautioned.

"What's Sambar compared to Civet?" The sergeant swam back up to eye level. "Didn't you leave him and his guard flat-footed?"

Slug nodded his head eagerly. "When do we leave?" He added with a slight bow of his head, "Your Highness."

I glared at Thorn, but he was hovering there proudly as if he didn't realize just what an awkward spot he had placed me in. Well, I suppose it was bound to come up sometime, but I would have preferred to tell just a few. As it was, I would just have to tough things out.

With a sigh, I chose my words carefully, trying not to lie and yet not wanting to discourage them. "I don't know. But the chief obstacle is gone now."

The sergeant jerked her head around on her long neck. "Will it take much to restore our home?"

Somehow Indigo managed to raise one brow ironically though I would have sworn a fish couldn't do it. Still, I suppose if there was a way, then the acid-tongued Indigo would find it. The old warriors were looking at me like so many simple children expecting a mage to pull gold coins out of nothing but air. I had to find a kinder way of letting them down than the truth: that I would be lucky to save the hides of myself and my two companions. I settled on a half-truth. "I—I haven't really thought about that," I stammered, hoping that they wouldn't hear the shame that was edging my voice. "At the moment, I'm just trying to keep my freedom."

"And," the sergeant declared proudly, "you've the clan to see to that now, Your Highness." She whirled around abruptly. "Wort," she ordered the one-eyed dragon, "go on ahead of us to the fort and tell them the great news."

"There's still a lot to be done," I warned them as they continued to celebrate. But in their own minds, they were already swimming in the waters of our ancient home. The more they built up their expectations, the harder would be the fall when I disappointed them—and disappoint them I would.

I looked at each of those grizzled veterans. Their faces and hides had as many scars and scratches as an old butcher's knife that's been honed and honed until there's almost nothing left of the knife. In fact, some of them were so maimed that they should not have been on active patrol. And yet each of them looked at me with all the eagerness and hope of dragons fresh from the egg. I wanted to give them something beyond empty assurances. After all these years of suffering and humiliation, they needed more than words. I reached into myself . . . and found nothing.

I was on the run, after all, with a magical pearl that I barely knew how to use. I was going to be lucky if I saved my own head, let alone my people. They deserved a real ruler—not some silly fool who thought ruling consisted of one banquet after another.

What was I going to do now?

CHAPTER ELEVEN

The undersea mountain rose like a lone sentinel squatting in the darkness. Coral grew upon its crown like brightly colored feathers on some helmet.

Thorn flicked his tail. "But where's the fort?"

"It's not like a human fort with a lot of walls." A kick of my legs sent me drifting forward another ten meters so that I was next to him. I nodded to the large holes about thirty meters from the surface. "Those are openings to a complex of rooms and tunnels. The garrison could stay in there for months until help came."

"And there are other openings disguised all around the mountain and the ridge so we could take the enemy from behind." The sergeant held up her claws. "These are a better defense than any human walls."

And then I saw the small mounds and markers on the slopes of the mountains near the edge of the visible light. "Even if it is more costly."

"But the High King doesn't care about the price." The sergeant flipped her paw open as if she were tossing a piece of trash over her shoulder. "So long as it's our clan that does the paying."

Ledges had been carved all around the mountain where long green streamers of seaweed could be grown. They drifted slowly like the veils of sleepy dancers. And off to the west, I could see dozens of large silver dots. One would flow westward for a while, then dissolve for several moments and then flow eastward.

Alarmed, Thorn darted in closer to me. After our run-in with the krakens, he was a little more cautious now. "What are those?"

"Our dinner, most likely." The sergeant impatiently signed to the rest of her squad to close up the intervals as they drifted up from the darkness. "Surely you of all creatures must have seen schools of fish before."

I spoke up for Thorn. "It's hardly likely since this is the first time he's seen an ocean. And there's no sense someone mistaking you for one of the school." I touched my forehead and worked the signs and muttered the spell that would change Thorn back into his true form.

The sergeant looked back and forth between the boy and myself. If she was surprised that Thorn might be more than some fishy servant, she hid it well as she changed her tone to a friendlier one while I changed Indigo back. "Well, you see, we train a few special ones to lead and the others always follow."

Thorn stretched his newly formed limbs. "You raise your own food too?"

Once her squad was separated by intervals of a meter or so, the sergeant joined us again with an almost leisurely motion of her forelegs. "The staples, at least. The other things have to come from the Rim. We're expected to be pretty self-sufficient."

The sergeant and her squad had picked up the pace now that they were so close to home. Thorn and Indigo could never have kept up with them with their puny human legs so I grabbed hold of their collars.

"Hey," Indigo tried to protest.

"Be quiet," I said as I dragged both of them

along like two heavy sacks. "This is faster."

Unfortunately, since I was doing all the work, Thorn had even more breath to chatter on the way humans will do. "But it sounds like they've just lumped you down in the middle of the sea."

The sergeant and her squad rose like a column of arrows rising in slow motion. At least two of them gave sad, bitter little laughs, but the sergeant chopped her paw through the water. "That's more accurate than you know, boy. We're the first of the forts that guards the forges."

Thorn wrapped his hands around my wrist to try to steady his motion as he was hauled through the sea. "How can you have forges in the sea?"

The sergeant tapped her steel-tipped claws sharply together this time so that they rang in a high, deadly note. "And where do you think these came from? It's dragon steel, boy. It never rusts and it never breaks. It's the truest of all metals."

Thorn stared at the glittering points on the sergeant's claws. "But you need fire to make steel."

The sergeant swept her paw to indicate the ridge below that was itself hidden in the darkness. "If you travel about fifty kilometers to the north along the Spine, you'll find a great undersea volcano, and it's in the fissures that the steel is forged. With all these rumors of war, they're working day and night."

"And I hope it's a war that never happens," I wished earnestly. It was nearly twilight on the surface now, and that was the time when the undersea villages really came to life. I watched as the farmers rose from the ledges where seaweed grew. Others left the banks of mussels near the surface. Over their shoulders were net sacks filled with the starfish that tried to eat the mussels—but which now in turn would be ground into meal to be fed to the fish.

The schools of fish were closer now, hurried on by the shepherds' calls, thinned and made shrill by the distance. The fish schools seemed to flicker like silver flames, vanishing and reappearing as they darted ever nearer to the safety of home. I glanced at the sergeant. "It reminds me of when I was a child and sometimes a servant would take me to visit a village."

"Were those happy times?" Thorn asked sympathetically.

"They certainly were the most peaceful that I can remember." And a kick of my legs sent me eagerly toward the fort.

Someone must have been keeping a lookout from

the mountain after the sergeant had sent on the messenger. The next thing I knew, hundreds of dragons came boiling out of the mountain, fanning outward like the plumes on a peacock's tail. Above them, the dying sun changed the surface of the sea from gold to red, and the last light gleamed on their scales.

The sergeant did a slow circle in the water as a happy courtesy to me. "Welcome, Your Highness. This may not be the High King's palace, but I think you'll find friendlier hearts here."

It was far more than I had expected and far more than I deserved. "I . . . I was just hoping for a meal and a little rest," I stammered.

"We owe far more to Your Highness than that. We thought you had died a long time ago in some faraway place." The sergeant crooked a claw and the clan swam toward us, forming a hollow tunnel. And when everyone was in position, the sergeant bowed for me to go on. "But now that you've made your way back to us, let us do what we can to make up for past wrongs."

And I realized that I hadn't waited all these years and traveled all this way to sit on a throne or eat a fancy banquet. All I had really wanted was to be among my own kind. For the first time in centuries, I felt as if I had finally come home.

When I hesitated, Thorn pulled free from my claws and swam over in front of me. "What's wrong?" he whispered.

I stared at the waiting dragons and my voice grew husky. "I was a fool to think a welcome from the High King meant anything. Even if he had actually had the trumpets blown for me and had spread out a feast, it could never have meant half as much as this welcome from my clan."

Thorn pulled at my snout encouragingly. "They're waiting."

It took me a moment to find my voice. I thought of these poor people waiting for some sign of hope—and all they had was me. "Yes. But they have a right to someone better than me."

Thorn swept his palm around toward the sergeant and her squad. "I don't hear any of them complaining."

I turned my head. What Thorn had said was true. From the pleased expressions on their faces, you would have thought I returned in triumph with a grand retinue of servants and soldiers instead of as I was: an outlaw fleeing the anger of the High King.

"Well, I can at least give them some sort of

spectacle." Impulsively, I reached my hand up to my forehead and uncovered the fold of flesh that hid the pearl. And its light went walking, walking through the waters—like long, tall stilts of silver. And the surrounding dragons seemed to breathe a collective sigh as they stared at the pearl.

And then, raising my tail as high as my head, I began to glide forward toward my clan.

"Welcome, Your Highness," one dragon murmured. Though he looked barely old enough to be hatched from the egg, his claws were tipped in steel as if he were already a warrior. With a chill, I remembered what the Grand Mage had said: Everyone in my clan was expected to "work." But I thought that children at least would be the exception.

"Bless you, child," mumbled another dragon who seemed old enough to be my grandmother. Despite that fact, her claws were also tipped with a warrior's steel. Apparently, everyone—from the youngest to the oldest—had to be prepared to fight. And though the silver light of the pearl seemed to soften the scars and wrinkles, it could not disguise the leanness of their bodies. And it could not hide the abuse they had suffered over the years.

Then someone released basketfuls of sea hares—small, frilly orange and red worms with comical tufts like land rabbits. But these were no bigger than one of my claws and they swarmed around me like a living shower of flowers.

"Thank you," I murmured. "Thank you." I was kept busy bowing to the left and to the right until I was almost dizzy. But I felt so much lighter inside—as if each smile and each heartfelt greeting were removing another of the many painful years I had spent in exile.

Toward the end of that living tunnel was an elderly dragon whose legs were bent as if they had been broken and never properly set. He shouldn't have been away from his bed, let alone trying to swim. Two younger dragons had to help hold him up. "We've waited so long for someone like you." Though the sea would swallow up any tears, he was blinking his eyes as if he were crying.

I could almost feel their warmth and affection reach out toward me like a giant hand that would take me up high above all my troubles so that nothing could ever harm me. "And I've waited a long time for something like this too." I bowed my head deeply to him.

"Now, there will be plenty of time to chat at the celebration." The sergeant swam up and took one of my legs. "In the meantime, we should all be getting back inside before it gets too dark."

But I had spent so many years alone that I had to pause in the entrance so I could blink the tears from my own eyes. Indigo, who had been following me at a safe distance, swam up to me now. "You're crying." She made it sound almost like an accusation.

"Something must have gotten into my eyes," I murmured as I hid the pearl once more.

"I suspect it's the season." The sergeant gave a snuffle herself. "There's a type of plankton that comes around that gets into everyone's sinuses."

The rooms in the mountain had been carved to be practical rather than ornate. On the walls and ceiling the rough edges had been left as if someone had been in a hurry to hollow out the mountain. It was so gloomy inside there that I felt almost as if I had stumbled inside a prison. And as I wiped my eyes, I saw huge chunks of dead coral used as shoring for parts of the corridor.

The sergeant saw the direction of my glance. "Seaquakes are a real problem here on the Spine.

We do what we can, but"—she shrugged—"it doesn't always work."

Some of the rooms had beds of barnacles on the walls and ceilings. The shells opened as our passing stirred the water. A lavender scallop jerked by on short jets of water. Light worms rose from their long, thin tubes, their petaled mouths casting a ghostly light. "You deserve better than this," I said fervently. "You shouldn't have to live in fear and darkness like this."

The sergeant stroked some of the worms in their tubes so that they glowed brighter for a moment. "We do our best, but it's a far cry from home."

Thorn and Indigo crouched to look down at someone's pet angler fish. The black, puffy fish used its fins to help it climb up the rocks while it dangled its glittering lure at them. "Why?" Thorn asked. "Because your old home was so peaceful?"

The worms had already grown dimmer. "No, we had our share of troubles, but our sea was shallow in many places so that the light reached to the sea floor, or almost to it. It was a place of light and life." I pounded my paw against a dark, barnacle-encrusted wall and felt the sharp edges of the shells dimly through my hide. But I knew that the darkness itself would have worn my soul away faster than the barnacles could wear through my hide. "It wasn't like this shadowy place at all."

"We're lucky to have this." The sergeant fell behind as she began to favor a leg with a deep scar.

I slowed deliberately. "How did that happen?"

The sergeant scratched her chin absently. "Oh, some skirmish with the krakens years ago. But the rheumatism's in the leg now."

I waved my paw back and forth, feeling the cold water swirl around it. "Yes, the water would be much colder than at home."

The sergeant shrugged fatalistically. "At least death here is a clean one. But many of our folk have to work at the forges. And the boiling water mixes with the sulfur fumes and makes an acid that eats at both your outsides and your insides." She paused beside a room that was only a little bigger than the cell back in Sambar's dungeons and only slightly better lit. "I'm sorry that we don't have anything better than this, Your Highness, but space is hard to come by in the fort. Some families have to take shifts on using rooms." She dipped her head apologetically. "I'm afraid we just don't have the time to carve out more space."

I thumped my tail against the door. "How could Uncle Sambar treat anyone this way?"

The sergeant took in a sharp mouthful of water and exhaled it slowly. "It's been difficult." She added, "Until now. But"—the sergeant bowed her head—"things will be different with you to lead us away from here. We've got a proper leader now—someone with some backbone."

The more I heard and saw the worse I felt. It would have been far kinder to have chained my clan within the dungeons than to condemn them to this place. Horrified, I began to suspect just what Civet's capture and my arrival meant to my clan. They expected me to rescue them all when I was going to be lucky to save myself and the two human children.

I placed a paw over the sergeant's mouth. "If I learned one thing in my travels, it's that it's better not to think on what might have been."

The sergeant pulled away. "Up until you came, a cold grave was all that we expected." She jerked a claw toward the lower slopes of the mountain where the cemetery was.

I lowered my head, reluctant to tell her that such an end might be all she could still anticipate. It was really a slow form of execution to leave them out here in this isolated outpost. What they needed was a proper home of their own again. But what could I do against the might of the High King? More than ever I knew I was no match for their enormous hopes. "You deserve a real princess," I blurted out, "not someone who's been living like a beggar all these years."

The squad stared at me in a puzzled way. That outburst just didn't fit in with their high image of me and they refused to give it up. I whirled around angrily so I could look at them each in turn. "Don't you understand? For the last few centuries, my main worry was how to get my next meal. I can't be the dragon you want me to be."

No one said anything for a long time; and then I felt the sergeant hook her leg through mine. "Do you think we want one of those brainless court nobles? Their main worry is what leg to use first when they start in a procession. We need someone tough—someone who's survived on her own without anyone else to help her."

I slid my leg free. "I don't think you would like the way I survived sometimes."

Thorn patted my shoulder. "The point is that you're resourceful or you wouldn't have gotten this far."

"B-but," I stuttered nervously, "I've just about run out of tricks. I don't know the first thing about leading dragons. The only thing I know how to do is plan a parade or a tournament or a masque."

However, the sergeant refused to be discouraged. "Listen to me, child. Sometimes you don't know what you really are until people start expecting things of you."

"But it's all wrong," I insisted. "I'm just going to disillusion you all."

The sergeant wagged a claw at me sternly. "It's not wrong to hope." She added with far more confidence than I felt, "You'll find a way, Your Highness."

I lifted my head slowly. Their faces were still so trusting. I could feel their faith surround me like a cloak that would keep away all those chilling sorts of doubts. I knew that I couldn't run away and leave them like this. "I'll get you home," I promised solemnly, "or I'll die trying."

CHAPTER TWELVE

Indigo made a face as she slid into the room. "It's like a dungeon cell."

Thorn swam in beside her. "But you know what your sentence is there. Here, you can die in a lot of different ways at any time."

As I shut the door, I kept hearing the Grand Mage's words echoing through my mind: "Where there's no spirit, there's no princess." It was time to pull myself together and do as the sergeant had suggested. "I can't leave them like this. I have to lead them away from here."

Indigo circled the room, "But you can't go up against Sambar and all his mages and his army."

I could feel all my clan's hopes and dreams weighing me down like a mountain. Desperately I tried to think of something I could do to help my people. I probably would need Baldy's cauldron to transport our sea back to its old place; and it wouldn't hurt to have Civet's help either—one way or another. But I didn't see how a refugee like me could get either one—unless I carried out Monkey's wild proposal. "The Lord of Flowers would be perfect if we could get his help. Walls mean nothing to him. It'd be child's play for him to get anything in the palace—Monkey, Civet or the cauldron."

"Is he that powerful?" Thorn set his back against a wall and stopped moving his limbs so that he simply settled to the floor.

I slumped against a wall while I tried to recall some of the stories. "He's so old that it's hard to separate legend from fact; but he's supposed to have been one of the first creatures to wake after the creation of the World. In fact, they say he's heard some of the songs of creation themselves."

Indigo swung her provisions sack to the floor and sat down in a corner. "We might as well wish for the stars as wish for a flower in the middle of an ocean."

"Well, are there any islands near here?" Thorn asked hopefully.

"It's still two hundred kilometers to the nearest island and that's to the east near the Abyss." I had come so far and suffered so much; and all I could do was to disappoint all the people who wanted to trust me. It would have been kinder if I had stayed away.

"I think I've had my fill of krakens, thank you." Indigo plumped up the sack to use as a pillow as she lay down. "But even if we had the flower, it's too dangerous to go back to the palace."

"No." I wagged a claw thoughtfully. "The last place they'd look for us is in the palace."

Indigo hugged herself. "That's because they assume you're smart. And anyway, what do you care? You don't owe these people anything. They turned their backs on you first." Indigo tightened her grip on herself. "Protect yourself first—that's my motto."

Thorn reached a hand over his shoulder and slapped his own scarred back. "Do you think you're the only one who's had a hard life? Her Highness and I have both had it rough."

"He didn't exactly have the kindest of masters," I added.

As if a lecture were almost as bad as a beating,

Indigo hardened her face into that familiar, hostile mask. "Then at least *he* ought to have some sense."

"We do." Thorn stuck out his legs. "We found that we're stronger together than we are separately." He glanced at me and grinned when he saw that we were both back in agreement together.

Indigo stared at him from the corners of her eyes. "How does that work?"

"An outlawed dragon and an orphan boy have more in common than you think." I tried to smile at her encouragingly. "We're both outcasts."

But all I received in answer was a scornful twist of her lip. "So what should I look for as my partner? A salamander?"

I kept my voice as gentle as I would if I were coaxing a sea hare to my finger. "It's not your fault that you haven't found friends in the past. If anyone's at fault, it's them."

Indigo didn't seem to know what to do with kindness. She scratched her cheek in a puzzled way. "It is?"

"Of course." I jabbed a claw at her to emphasize my words. "You're capable of feeling and doing anything that any other creature can."

Indigo dropped back on her heels. "You're a strange one—all those centuries in exile and you still haven't given up."

"So maybe this is all mad"—I shrugged—"but let me tell you something, child. I've been alone most of my life and during that time I've been the most practical person around—and yet I've never felt as good and as strong as I do now."

Thorn flung out an exasperated hand. "Friends are important. You don't run out on them just when they're fighting for their lives."

There was just the slightest guilty pause before Indigo snapped, "I left because I want to live."

"Who calls that living?" Thorn sniffed.

"I don't fool myself with crazy schemes like you do." Indigo spoke with less conviction than before. "Just like you are right now."

I sighed, because I might as well have tried to teach her how to fly when she was in human form. "Sometimes dreams make people rise above their own selfish interests. Dreams make people better."

Indigo's eyes flicked away while she tried to think of something to say; but for the first time since I'd met her, she seemed at a loss for words. And I took that as a good sign. If I could make her understand certain things, then perhaps I wouldn't really have wasted all those years of wandering, after all.

But before I could say anything more, a steel-tipped claw tapped at the door. "Your Highness?" the sergeant asked.

I rose to my feet. "Yes, come in."

The door swung open again but the sergeant only poked her head in through the doorway. "We can't do much to make this seem like home, but we'll try."

From the corridor, musicians began to play a song that I had not heard in centuries—the Weaver's Lament, which describes his sorrow at leaving his home to fight the krakens. Bows slid over the strings of moon fiddles and claws beat at drums made from hide stretched over hoops. It was a song as much of hope and faith in the future as it was about sadness.

I was almost in tears at this point. "Music too?"

"A little concert." The sergeant smiled as if she were immensely pleased by my reaction.

"Don't jabber on so," said an old dragon in the corridor. "The poor child is likely to die of hunger while you make your speeches."

With a laugh, the sergeant stepped back. "Some of your people thought you might be hungry from your journey."

They came one by one to the door—some of them silver with age, others almost newly hatched from eggs—each with a stone tray on which was some delicacy. Slivers of raw fish sliced into the shape of flowers, shelled limpets with a garnish of seaweed and other such dishes.

But the best was brought by the last dragon, an elderly male by the name of Bulbul. He had brought a whole tray filled with jelly cakes. They would have been mixed on the surface and then carried in a covered pot down into the lower depths where the cold would congeal the ingredients. I certainly appreciated all the work that went into it.

"Thank you." I raised my head with all the regalness that I had been taught. "After all these years of wandering, this meal will taste far better than anything I ever had within my father's palace. I . . . I don't know what to say to such kindness."

Bulbul knelt sheepishly. "Bless you, Your Highness, but the clan has three treasures now because of you."

I wrinkled my forehead in puzzlement because I could account for only one—the dream pearl. "Three treasures?"

Bulbul raised one paw and crooked one claw against the flat of his paw. "There's the dream pearl." He bent a second claw. "The flower." He folded a third claw and smiled shyly. "And you— our long-lost little princess."

I suppose I should have been enjoying the fact that everyone was nodding their head in agreement with Bulbul, but I'm afraid my mind was taken up by something else he'd said. "Flower?" I exchanged glances with Thorn; and even Indigo sat up excitedly.

Bulbul lowered his paw to the floor. "I picked it on the shore myself the day before the Witch came. It was a stalk of Ebony's tears. The very same flowers that grew when he was in exile and weeping for his lost love."

While I didn't pay much attention to the story, I remembered the little flowers that had bloomed all around the shores of the Inland Sea so that sometimes our sea had seemed surrounded by low-hanging clouds. "They were always so fragrant."

Bulbul nodded his head as he saw that I understood. "My wife loved them so much that I asked my sister, who was a mage, to preserve it with a spell. And I brought it here myself."

I gripped his foreleg eagerly. "Is your sister here?"

"No, Your Highness." He shook his head with a distant sorrow. "She perished with my wife and so many other fine dragons that terrible night when the Witch came." He patted the paw that held her. "But at least I have the flower."

"It still gives off a scent after all these years," the sergeant added with a wistfulness that I hadn't expected in her. It was nice to see that such fragile emotions still existed despite the clan's harsh life. "Sometimes, when I close my eyes, I can almost see the shores of the Inland Sea."

"Unfortunately, the flower isn't mine anymore. It's become the symbol of our lost home. It belongs to the entire clan. We each take turns guarding it. Right now it's at the forges"—Bulbul shifted on his hind legs to look at the sergeant—"but maybe we could ask them to send the flower to us."

The sergeant plucked at her lip thoughtfully. "I don't know. That branch of the clan always insists on its rights."

"This is for Her Highness." Bulbul indignantly slapped his paw on her foreleg.

"But they haven't met her." The sergeant shoved his paw away.

However, my mind was already remembering our previous conversation. Maybe this flower was just the thing we needed to help Monkey—and perhaps ourselves. I was desperate enough to try anything to help my people now. "Must the entire clan vote on who is to have the flower?"

"No"—Bulbul turned back to me and dipped his head—"that is up to whichever branch of the clan is the guardian."

I slipped a jelly cake into my paw. I hadn't had that particular delicacy in ages and it tasted heavenly. "And they would decide?"

Bulbul wagged a paw, urging me to take another. "That branch of the clan follows the lead of one person: Lady Francolin. And she's very jealous about the guardianship." He added kindly, "They have so little, after all."

The name sounded familiar and I frantically searched my memory. I dimly remembered her as a history tutor at my father's court. As I recalled, I'd thought her a boring old horror then. But she must be positively ancient by now. I wasn't sure if she would grant me any favors, but I had to try.

I turned my head in a dignified way to look at the sergeant and Bulbul. "Then what if I went to the forges myself?"

Bulbul spread out his paws in alarm. "Your Highness can't be serious. No one goes there if they can help it."

I took one of his paws in mine. "Bulbul, I must have that flower for the good of the clan."

His eyes searched my face alertly. "Your Highness has a plan?"

"Or the start of one." I squeezed his paw. "It might mean the destruction of the flower, though."

Bulbul hesitated as he slid his paw away from mine. "Will it help us get home?"

I dropped my paw helplessly to my lap. "I hope so. At least I might gain a powerful friend."

Pressing his lips together, he nodded his head bravely. "Then use it as you will, Your Highness."

The sergeant gave a skeptical snort. "She still has to convince Lady Francolin to surrender the flower."

But I was feeling more hopeful now that there

was a remote possibility. "That's right. Let's tackle one problem at a time."

We got off to an early start the next morning with the sergeant and her squad as our escorts. The sergeant had a sack of mussels and each of the squad had some small sack or shell. The sergeant hefted her own sack. "The guards at the forges would be suspicious if we didn't bring presents."

Nodding my head in agreement, I disguised Thorn and Indigo as middle-aged dragons this time. The sergeant eyed my work critically. "Look at their clean hides. They'd never fit into my squad."

"Then let's do it right." I placed a few scars artistically and then lengthened my own snout slightly and enlarged my eyes. I held out one of my scarred legs. "Do these pass inspection?"

"They'll do." She touched several scars on one shoulder. "But these were never made by any creature's claws or fangs."

I shoved the sergeant's claws away. "No, it was the lash. I haven't always had my first choice in disguises and occupations."

The forges themselves were only some fifty kilometers away from the fort; and the trip itself was uneventful until we neared the forges themselves.

As we swam downwards, the darkness began to lighten. "What's happening?" Thorn held up a paw and wriggled his claws. "I can see again."

"We're getting near the undersea volcanoes." I watched as a huge-jawed fish swam by leisurely. A glowing bit of flesh dangled in front of it to attract other fish who would think it was a smaller sea creature. "The heat makes it possible for the plankton to bloom again."

"And what's that smell?" Thorn waved his paw in front of his snout.

"It's sulfur," the sergeant explained. "It comes from the volcanoes."

"Who's there?" A dragon shot upward from behind an outcropping and about a half-dozen dragons rose behind him. He had all the arrogance of a Deep dragon—one of those who are born and bred in the seas and who think of themselves as the purest and best of the dragons.

The sergeant dipped her head in sullen respect. "Just bringing a message to some of our kin, sir."

The dragon raised a languid paw and I could see the disk around his neck. It had the single circle of an ensign. "Don't you have better things to do than to go scurrying about visiting your kin?"

The sergeant started to draw the forged wax pass from the sack hanging from her neck. "We all have leave, sir. It's been months—"

"Yes, yes." The ensign waved his claws imperiously. "That's what all your kind say. Go on." And, signing to his patrol beneath him, he swam away.

The sergeant waited until the ensign was out of sight. "That kind never lives long on the Spine."

"Why don't they live any longer than you?" Thorn looked off in the direction that the ensign had taken.

The sergeant drew her lips back in a nasty little smile. "Because they meet with 'accidents.' "

Thorn's eyes widened. "You kill them?"

The sergeant snapped at him impatiently. "It's a matter of self-protection. An idiot like that ensign can get all of his soldiers killed."

I swam between the sergeant and Thorn just in case Thorn said the wrong thing. "I can understand that," I said quickly. I was sure it was a touchy subject with them. "But don't they send out replacements?"

The sergeant gave a chuckle. "The generals used to, but when officers kept meeting with accidents, the fort lost its appeal. Every now and then they try to send out some officer to take charge, but most of the time they're satisfied as long as we keep the krakens away from their front doors."

Thorn swam a bit away from the sergeant. "That sounds harsh."

"It's a harsh life, boy," the sergeant said and added, "and getting harsher all the time."

CHAPTER THIRTEEN

We passed over the peaks of the undersea mountain range, their tops round as melted candy. Then, far in the distance, we saw a bright, thin flash of light as if someone had just drawn a stroke with a fiery pen. There was a kind of afterimage left on my eyes long after the light itself had vanished. "Was that one of the volcanoes?"

The sergeant studied the spot. "No, it was probably a vent letting off pressure. The magma builds underneath the volcanoes and the engineers try to let it out through side vents before it can erupt."

"And that controls it?" Thorn slowed.

"Most of the time." The sergeant swam along with an easy side stroke. "But the engineers are guessing at best. There was a small eruption about a hundred years ago. It killed ten of our people."

"But what about recently?" Thorn gulped.

"It hasn't gone off in a while, but I won't make any promises that the volcanoes won't erupt when we're there." The sergeant snatched at a yellow slug whose flat, rippling body looked like a bright handkerchief waving in the water. She offered it first to me; and when I declined, she held the squiriming slug out to Thorn and Indigo. They shook their heads so violently that they raised small streamers of bubbles. "Your uncle has given us fine choices, hasn't he, Your Highness? It's either sit on top of a mountain that's about to blow up underneath us or have krakens for neighbors."

Even though I still wasn't sure what I could do against the might of the High King, I forced myself to smile. "I'll see what I can do about giving you more choices."

There was no one central fort to protect the forges, but instead there were small outposts on the mountains to the north and south and on seamounts—old, collapsed volcanoes to the west and east. Puzzled, I turned to the sergeant. "Why are the guards scattered at all the posts like this?"

The sergeant popped the slug into her mouth and chewed it without pleasure. "They're more worried about riots among the workers than they are about attacks by the krakens. The generals count on an early warning from the outposts to meet any invasion."

A faint tinkling sound came from broad ledges below. As we dropped toward them, the tinkling grew to a steady, rhythmic ringing of hammers on metal.

The vents themselves showed as angry, twisted smiles of fire through the clouds of steam; but we could see long lines of dragons streaming into them. The sergeant pointed at the baskets of iron ore and coal that were on some of the workers' backs. "Other branches of the clan mine the ore."

"I imagine that has its own hazards," I said as I watched other dragons emerge with red, glowing bars of steel.

They brought them to the wide ledge where the dragonsmiths waited. There, the smiths and their apprentices would pound the steel and work their spells before the metal cooled too much. Often, they could only manage a few blows before the bar had to be returned to the vent to be heated again. But all around that ledge, steel was being shaped for claws, spearheads and even large rams that would be used to sink whatever human ships tried to sail out of the harbor.

However, the sergeant stopped me when I tried to swim closer. "This is far enough. Sulfur gases from the vents mix with water to form acid." She gestured for us to follow her away from there.

When we left the forges, I could see why the workers might riot. Though the guard posts were tunnels in the mountain peaks, the workers themselves lived in miserable little huts built out of slabs of rock on ledges or anchored over crevices. The earthquakes that damaged the fort would probably be even more dangerous here. I could have wept for my people if it wouldn't have revealed my true identity.

As it was, I was glad when we went directly to one little shack and the sergeant tapped her claws at the stone door. A young dragon opened the door. His scales were pitted and there were even a few missing so that his raw skin was exposed. "It's Chukar, Auntie," he announced.

The sergeant wriggled the back of her paw at her squad and they seemed to drift off among the huts as if to rest or to visit. But I noticed they all kept our hut in sight. In the meantime, the sergeant had put a broad smile on her face. "We've brought fresh mussels for Lady Francolin."

"She's not feeling well; but I'll save them for later." The youngster tried to snatch the sack from the sergeant.

"I've brought some clan members a long way to see her." The sergeant held the sack just out of reach.

"Thrush, visitors are always welcome—especially if they bring mussels." The voice was high and thin but not unpleasant—like a flute played by an old musician who may have all her old skills but not quite the breath anymore.

"You're only supposed to have kelp," Thrush scolded gently. He looked in appeal to the sergeant. "She didn't hold her breath at the forges, and the sulfuric acid ruined her insides."

"But my stomach's less tender now," Lady Francolin countered. "I don't think one mussel would hurt. Let them in."

"You're going to have to squeeze in then." Thrush grudgingly backed into the hut.

A kind of green luminescent coral that looked like a sheet of bubbles had been encouraged to grow on the walls. But there were large patches of dark yellow where the coral had died. Still, there was enough light to see a plain but pleasant room—though all the items looked as if they had been scavenged from various trash piles at the soldiers' outposts.

Against one wall was a long, low stone table that was missing one leg so a block of granite took its place. The bowls and utensils on top of the table had cracks or chips and the stone cabinet was missing one door, though someone had woven sea kelp into a kind of curtain to hang in place of the absent door.

Stooping, I peered through the doorway. A dragon with scales of a silvery white lay in one corner. Her hide was just as pitted and broken as Thrush's; but some disease had withered her legs so that they barely seemed capable of supporting her. I gaped in disbelief. "Surely they don't expect you to work too."

"I clean away scraps mostly." She gave a shrug that said far more about courage than a hundred speeches. "We each do what we can," she quavered. "But I needn't tell you that. Any of the clan of the Lost Sea is welcome. However, I'll expect you to pay."

I eased into the hut. "Pay?"

"With your story, child." She nodded for me to take a spot near her. "I'm trying to put together an oral history of the clan—especially if you have any memories of the night when the Witch came."

I was feeling a bit guilty that I had only thought of my history tutor as an old horror. Right now she seemed like a far more interesting person than I remembered. But then court life had a way of distorting people. "Of course," I agreed.

She smiled apologetically. "I'm afraid an old dragon must have something to justify living."

The sergeant set the mussels down in front of her. "Oh, now, where would the clan be, Auntie, without your long memory?"

"Perhaps moving ahead instead of looking backward." Lady Francolin kept a tight hold on the sack.

The sergeant motioned for the others to squeeze into the hut though we were packed shoulder to shoulder, and a grumbling Thrush had to climb over us to shut the door once again before he perched on top of the table. "My," the sergeant said, "you're in quite a mood."

Lady Francolin sighed. "It's just that with this

war scare on, we seem ever further away from returning to the Inland Sea."

The sergeant reached into the sack and whispered confidently, "Not anymore. The Witch has been captured."

I could only guess at the physical cost as Lady Francolin reared her head up. "How. When?"

The sergeant used the tips of her claws to pry the shell apart. "Do you remember the Princess Shimmer?"

When the sergeant passed the mussel to the Lady, Thrush cleared his throat noisily. With a small pout, the Lady waved the mussel away. "Naturally. I always felt bad that we let that poor little thing be driven off. She was so young when she took that pearl."

The words came from me automatically. "Her mother left it to her, not to her brother."

Though the Lady's legs might be nearly useless, her mind wasn't. "Come closer, child." It was hard to move around in that already overcrowded hut; but when I managed to lean forward, she wrinkled her forehead as her eyes explored my face. "There's something about you that . . ." Her voice drifted as she tried to puzzle it out.

And I saw not the invalid dragon before me, but a dragon who had stood over me years before, scolding me in a passionate, almost desperate voice. "A very stubborn young dragon once told you that she didn't want to learn history because it was boring. And you told her that history was like a great beast that one either learned how to ride or got trampled by."

With difficulty Lady Francolin raised a foreleg and passed a paw over her face. "Yes, I recall something like that, but it was so long ago." Her paw suddenly dropped and she looked at me in shock. "Your Highness."

"Now that stubborn little dragon *makes* history." The sergeant swallowed the mussel herself. "She caught Civet."

The Lady sat there stunned. "But where did you get the army to capture the Witch?"

I touched Thorn's neck. "I just needed one friend." Indigo looked at him with new curiosity as if she didn't expect it of him.

"But this is wonderful." In her delight, the Lady almost knocked the entire sack over. "Thrush, call the others—"

"No." I pressed my paw over her mouth. I'd

often wished that I could do that when I'd been a child; but I'd never thought I'd have the opportunity. "No one must know of my visit until after I'm gone. I'm a fugitive from the High King." I lowered my paw. "He wanted to take the dream pearl."

"Greed is going to do in Sambar yet. It's the one vice that cannot be tolerated in a High King." She slowly wriggled her claws at me as if she could pull the words from my mouth. "But hurry. Tell me your tale, child."

Quickly, Thorn and I outlined our adventure within Civet's mountain, our meeting with Indigo and our subsequent little swim through Sambar's kingdom.

When I was finished, Lady Francolin slowly raised her withered foreleg. It trembled as she tried to extend it toward me. "I have the feeling that you haven't told us half of what you suffered during your exile. And your wandering must continue."

I took her paw in mine. "There is something you can do; and it's not just for me but for the entire clan—though some of your folk may not understand."

I felt her claws squeeze mine. "What is it, Your Highness?"

I took in a deep lungful of water and let it out slowly. "I need the flower if I'm to gain powerful allies."

"But that's all that keeps some of the older ones going," Thrush protested from the table. "They sit and smell the flower and remember; and the young ones listen."

I twisted my head around to face him. "I don't ask for it lightly. I must have the flower if I'm to restore the sea." I realized that *restore* was the wrong word to use as soon as I said it.

It was hard to see someone as tough as the sergeant suddenly sag. "You mean it's gone?"

Lady Francolin looked at me in disbelief; but it was the sergeant who spoke. "You mean those lovely gardens?"

I would rather have walked over a road of sharp knives than do what I had to now. But I had to be truthful. "Everything's gone—the palace too."

I looked hastily between Lady Francolin and the demoralized sergeant. "I'll be honest with you because I think you're strong enough to hear the truth. The wind and the weather have destroyed almost everything on the sea floor. But if we can bring back the sea, I think we can restock the sea life and rebuild things."

"How can we match the architects in your grandfather's time?" The sergeant wondered.

But Lady Francolin looked more rebellious. "The palace was built to last a thousand years. I don't believe you."

"Don't or won't?" I asked her quietly. "I know these dreams have kept you going so I don't ask you to give them up lightly. But you have to understand why I need the flower."

Of the soldier and the teacher, it was Lady Francolin who was the tougher and who recovered first. "You . . . you'll return it?"

"I can't promise anything," I said, "because I don't know how it's to be used."

The Lady looked down at her claws as she rubbed the tips together. "But it's all we have left of the Inland Sea."

"You just said it was time to move forward," Thorn argued. "You might lose one flower, but you might regain a home."

"You're asking us to risk a good deal." The Lady rested her forelegs on the floor for a moment and then nodded quietly to Thrush. "Show it to them."

"But Grandmother—" Thrush tried to object.

Lady Francolin reared her head imperiously as if she were no longer an old dragon in a miserable hut but was once more a royal tutor. "Show them," she commanded. "They must realize what they're asking us to give up."

Reluctantly, Thrush rose to his haunches and reached over to the cabinet and jerked back the curtain and then opened the door. When I was a child, I had never paid much attention to those little flowers; but now my eyes savored every detail.

The last of Ebony's tears sat within a simple stone vase; and from the slender stalk sprang a half-dozen clusters of small pinwheel-shaped flowers. "They're as white as I remember them," I murmured, and I drew in as much water as I could through my nostrils—and it seemed as if I could make out the faint scent that still rose from the stalk. "It brings back memories of sunny afternoons by the shore." I smiled sadly at the memory. "We used to roll down whole slopes of them and dive into the water. We must have crushed this kind of flower by the thousands."

Indigo rose eagerly. "Is that what a flower looks like? It's better than my parents described."

Lady Francolin, who knew Indigo was a disguised human, smiled kindly at her. "Then you must have lived most of your life in the palace if you've only heard about the beauties of the land."

Indigo clicked her claws together nervously. "Besides Thorn, this"—she pointed at the flower— "is the first thing I've ever seen from the mainland."

Lady Francolin clicked her tongue sympathetically. "Then you're an exile and that makes you kin in a way."

Indigo put on her cautious, masklike expression. "What do you mean?"

Lady Francolin pursed her lips together in a sad little smile. "We are also far from home."

Indigo rocked back on her haunches sullenly. "But you don't really know what it's like to be *that* alone."

"That's true," Lady Francolin conceded with a dip of her head, "but the princess would. In fact, she has endured an exile far greater than yours."

Startled, Indigo gave me a sideways glance. I guess that she had never thought about the similarities between us so I smiled at her encouragingly. "My homecoming is just going to be a little more complicated than yours."

With the graciousness of an old courtier, Lady Francolin motioned for Thrush to lift the flower from the cabinet and bring it closer to us. "You must have a better look at this flower; for you won't find its like anywhere on the mainland now. These grew only on the shores of the Inland Sea; and this is the last."

Thrush stretched his body forward over Thorn and then Indigo. Indigo touched one of the petals wonderingly and then snatched back her claws as if afraid she would break the lovely thing. "I wouldn't part with it if it was mine," she declared fervently.

"The old ones like to sit and reminisce about it." Thrush looked at me almost accusingly as if I were going to snatch that from them. "And the young ones like to listen and imagine they're away from the forges. What right do you have to take that away from us?"

"Shh," Lady Francolin hushed him. "We can't just sit and talk about the old days. We have to see about making a set of new days." She added hopefully, "Perhaps you could take just one flower from the stalk—or even just leave us one flower."

"I'd like to," I sighed. "But I don't know how many flowers I'll need."

Thrush set the flower back within the cabinet. "I know she caught the Witch, but restoring the sea sounds even harder. Is she the one to do it?"

"Have more respect for Her Highness." The sergeant would have hooked a foreleg around the youngster's neck, but I stopped her.

"No, he has a right to ask," I corrected her quietly, and then I looked straight at Thrush. "I can only promise you that I will try my best, but even that hasn't always been enough."

Lady Francolin cupped a trembling paw around my chin and held it so she could look straight into my eyes. In the distance, we could hear the faint clinks of the smiths' hammers at the forge; but at the moment I felt as if I were being weighed against all those heroic kings and queens that filled her memory.

I didn't think the comparison would be very flattering, so I was surprised when she raised her head and her voice grew as passionate as it had once been in the schoolroom. "But I think that each failure has only made you stronger. You plunged your soul into the next adventure the way a smith would temper a blade: thrust it into the fire and take it out and pound it again and then thrust it back into the fire once more. That's what makes dragon steel so strong. It is tempered long and often. And each time it is thrust into the fire and beaten, it only gets harder." She let her paw drop. "You may have the flower, Your Highness."

"Really?" Indigo seemed impressed by that sacrifice.

"But it's all we have, Grandmother," Thrush tried to protest.

Lady Francolin silenced him with a curt nod of her head. "She won't fail, I tell you. She's like steel—dragon steel."

CHAPTER FOURTEEN

Bubbling over with more hope than I had felt in ages, we left the Lady Francolin. The sergeant escorted us some twenty kilometers from the forges—which was about as far as she dared go. She and her squad drew up in a crescent formation in front of us. "Heaven speed your trip and protect you at its end," she wished fervently.

Though I had been with her for only a short time, I knew that I would miss her rough, quiet strength. For the first time in months—maybe even in years—I had felt safe. Dragons like her formed the backbone of any clan. "I'll send word when I can," I promised, "but it may take a long time."

The sergeant bowed her head. "We'll be waiting."

I raised the sack that held the boxed flower as

a salute to them. "We'll dance in the Inland Sea yet." But I froze as I saw the dragons swiftly descending toward us.

As they drew closer, I recognized the ensign who had questioned us on the way to the forge. "It's the same patrol that stopped us before."

"Leave this to us, child." I suppose she was afraid of having someone overhear my title. The sergeant drifted overhead with a kick of her legs. "And if I tell you and your friends to swim, you swim." And the rest of her squad followed her so that they were between us and the oncoming dragons.

"State your business," the ensign ordered. He and his squad swam in deadly spirals like hawks.

The sergeant dipped her head. "Going home from a visit to our kin, sir."

The ensign dropped a little lower. "The last time I saw you, you were coming from the eastern fort." He signed to his squad and they fanned out. "Why are you lying? What are you ungrateful scum up to?"

"Get away, child." The sergeant knocked me even lower with a lash of her tail and then rose with her squad toward the ensign.

"I can't run out on you," I said, and tried to follow.

But the sergeant and her squad went on thrashing upward, rising in huge columns of silver bubbles that their legs and tails churned up. "We'll make mincemeat out of these fat garrison troops."

However, the ensign and his squad were diving like determined old veterans so I had my doubts. "Then this won't delay me too long."

Slug dropped out to block my way. "This is our gift to you and to our clan. Don't spoil it."

"Yes," the sergeant growled from above, "don't be so selfish and hog all the glory."

And I slowed in the water. While I still felt a little guilty about letting someone else do my fighting for me, I had to admit that they had a point. It wasn't just me or them anymore, but the future of our entire people. It was an even heavier burden than I had thought.

Behind me I could hear Thorn giving the war cry of our clan. While I knew that he had a brave enough heart, he had never fought in the form of a dragon. "Good luck," I called after them.

The sergeant waved her paw in farewell.

Thorn paused beside me, puzzled. "Aren't we going to fight?"

"No, we've more important things to do." I looked around for Indigo and saw her moping along below at a safe distance—as usual. "Come along," I said, and I started to swim toward the west. But I stopped after a hundred meters to look back at the swirling, churning figures. The ensign's squad might have been garrison troops, but they knew how to fight. I couldn't help wondering just who would become the mincemeat. With a sigh, I turned and kicked my legs so that I would move forward once again.

It was the first time in ages that I had followed someone else's wishes. And it was hard.

We had gone two kilometers before a thoroughly puzzled Indigo wriggled in front of us with a graceful arching of her body. "First, they gave up the flower. Now some of them are giving up their lives. And yet they could have gotten a lot more by turning you in." She seemed genuinely puzzled.

Thorn pulled himself through the water with long, easy strokes so that he could pace himself. "They used to say in my village that dreams were the best magic of all. They could change mud into gold sometimes."

"But not often." Indigo swam with short, choppy

strokes as if her mind were only half on swimming.

Thorn straightened out his neck and began to
kick with all four legs until he was beside her again.
"You have to believe in something sometime."

Indigo shot an indignant look over her shoulder.
"I do. I believe in the Green Darkness."

Thorn slapped the water. "That's not faith; that's
just selfishness."

Indigo drew away stiffly. "Well, it suits me."

Again, I had the eerie feeling that I was looking
in a mirror. So as much for my own sake as for
hers, I tried to explain. "You're not going to have
that forest to yourself. You'll have to get along
with others."

Indigo missed a stroke as if that had never oc-
curred to her. "I'll survive. I always do."

I craned my neck forward to make sure she
could hear my urgent words. "There's more to life
than just surviving. That's why people are willing
to sacrifice treasures like the flower—or even their
lives."

Indigo's legs slowed and then stopped alto-
gether. Her head turned this way and that as if
she were lost and looking for a signpost; but she

refused to look at either of us. "I want to believe you two. I do. I really do. But it goes against so much of what I know."

Thorn's face softened. It was difficult for him to hold a grudge against even the meanest person. "You may have left that kitchen in body but you haven't left it in spirit."

Indigo still kept her eyes straight ahead of her. It was hard for her to admit that she could make any sort of mistake because that was also being weak. "Maybe," she admitted reluctantly, and then sighed. "I don't know. Things used to be so clear before I met you two. Now everything seems so muddied."

We took our time as we approached the gardens; but there didn't seem to be any of the guard about. I suppose they were still off chasing our shadows. In the distance, a few gardeners simply went on with their work. No one noticed us swimming toward an abandoned music room.

There were still little divans where the musicians would have squatted, and on one of them was a drum whose torn hide partially covered the hoop; but silt had settled in a fine film over everything and barnacles grew on the walls so that in the dim light they looked as if they were covered with black wool.

"Here." I handed the sack with the box to Thorn. "I want both my paws free for fighting."

"So do I," Thorn said, but he took the box anyway.

In the meantime, Indigo had been peering out into the corridor. "It's all right. It's safe." She motioned us out into the corridor and led us past more silent, abandoned rooms until we reached the storage rooms by the kitchen once again. She motioned us into one of them and shut the door again.

"What we'll have to do," she whispered, "is ambush the servants who bring food to the dungeons. Once we get them out of the way, you can disguise us to look like them."

"And the guards?" Thorn wondered.

"We'll just have to take our chances." She pinched Thorn's cheek. "But I'm sure a cutey like you will be able to charm them."

Thorn moved to a safe distance as he rubbed his face. "Not if they hit that hard."

We spent several hours in the storage room. Now that she was back near her old home, Indigo

had become a bit more talkative about her past—
as if the talking could keep old ghosts away.

Her mother had died shortly after they had come
to the palace. They said it was of heart failure,
but her father had always insisted that it was a
lack of sunshine. Then, four years ago, her father
had died when a set of shelves in one of the storage
rooms had fallen on him. His body had barely
turned cold before their fellow servants had stripped
their room of its few furnishings and their belongings.

From that day on, Indigo had been the victim
of a type of random and casual cruelty. None of
the other servants went out of their way to be
mean to the strange child; but they thought nothing of stealing her meager rations or of beating her
when they wanted to take their anger out on someone—until the day that Indigo had snatched up a
meat cleaver and threatened to take off the paw
of a dishwasher who had tried to steal her dinner.

From then on, she had never slept in the servants' quarters for fear of getting caught but had
slept elsewhere in the palace, returning to the
kitchen so she could do the work that would earn
meals for her.

"And in the meantime you dreamed of the Green Darkness," I said.

She settled back against the stone side of a crate. "Sometimes it doesn't seem like a dream. Sometimes I almost think I can see it." She arched her head back, exposing her throat. "I can see the green leaves far above like the surface of a sea."

"Well—" I began when Thorn held up a paw. "Someone's coming."

I winked at Indigo. "Let's hope it's someone with whom you've got to settle a score."

As we took our positions by the door, we could hear the heavy wheels of the cart rolling down the corridor. "Ready?" I asked them.

Indigo wrapped her claws into two leathery balls. "I've been ready for four years to have a body like this."

Thorn jerked the door open at my nod, and we darted out into the corridor. There were two servants this time with the food cart. One of them was a squat little dragon who looked more like a toad than a dragon. He was pushing the cart. The other was a lanky, beanpole type who was moping after the cart as if he didn't enjoy this detail.

"Take the other one," I yelled, and shot over the head of the squat one.

Beanpole tried to crouch and raise his legs over his head, but he was already too late. My paw thudded at the base of his skull and he slumped to the floor.

From behind me, I could hear muffled screams, and I turned to see Thorn with his paws wrapped around the squat dragon's mouth while Indigo pounded away at his skull. Hammering on a skull probably helped her take out a lot of her anger, but it would never knock out that one.

I put one paw to Thorn's shoulder so that he drifted to the side a little and left me room to swing. A quick chop to the base of the squat dragon's skull left him sprawled on the corridor floor.

"Hurry." Indigo had grabbed one of the squat dragon's forelegs. Thorn took the other and I took the hind legs, and together we slowly dragged him toward the storage room.

"At least someone must like the cook's food," I grunted.

"He ought to be fat. He used to take enough of my meals." Indigo was looking down with satisfaction at the unconscious dragon.

When we had him inside the storage room, we went out for the beanpole. Strange to say, he was even harder to carry than the squat one. I don't know whether it was heavy bones or just his length that made him such an awkward burden, but it took us even longer to dump him into the storage room.

"This one doesn't like to eat?" I took out the coil of kelp that we had found in the storage room.

Indigo picked up another coil of kelp. "No, this one uses up all his energy beating up younger, smaller servants."

As soon as we had them bound and gagged, I stood up, slapped my paws together. "Thorn and I can pretend to be them."

"No, I have to talk to the guards and it'll be better if I'm in the shape of someone that they know." She kicked the squat one. "Make me like him."

It took only a moment to change her into the squat one and myself into the beanpole. Thorn would just stay in his own shape as a kind of helper.

When we were finished, I took out the box and lifted off the lid. The room was filled with the scent of that long-vanished shore. I stared at the flower for a moment. "It brings back so many memories."

Indigo went outside into the corridor, lifted the lid from one plate and dumped the contents into the storage room. "I hope that one flower is enough."

I put the flower onto the plate and let Indigo slam the lid back down. "We'll find out soon enough, won't we?" I said.

CHAPTER FIFTEEN

The guard at the dungeon door was the same wide-haunched one that had let us out. He was as charming as ever. "Well, what did you bring us this time, boys?"

"Nothing." The disguised Indigo tried to ram the cart past him, but he stuck out a hind leg to block it.

"Why is it that the prisoners get their meals more regularly than the guards?" he demanded.

"Because you have to eat when the other servants do." Indigo tried to angle the cart around the hind leg, but the guard slid forward so that his leg could still block her.

"And by the time you lie-abouts finish eating and get around to serving us our meals, we're half-starved." He lifted the lid from one plate, frowned and slammed the lid back down.

Indigo nudged his hind leg with the cart. "I don't make the rules. Look, don't get me into trouble."

There was a second guard now—I suppose as extra security. He had a broad scar across his lips. "Trouble. You don't know what that is until you let some prisoners escape."

The first guard raised another lid. "Any word on that Indigo?"

The second guard placed his paws one above the other and pretended to wring something. "Oh, wouldn't I just love to strangle that little traitor for causing us so much misery. Double watches and half-pay."

Indigo couldn't resist rubbing it in. Apparently she had been given most of the credit for the escape. "You shouldn't have been so careless."

It was the wrong thing to say. The first guard stiffened and held the lid like a shield. "Well, maybe we ought to be more careful now. You never know what contraband might be slipped to the prisoners—knives, keys and Heaven knows what else." He deliberately took a shrimp from the plate and ate it.

Indigo glanced at the number on the lid. "I don't think the prisoner in Cell 81 is going to like that."

"I don't think he's got much choice." The first guard put the lid down and took several leaves of red kelp and crunched them down.

The second guard got caught up in the spirit of the thing. "This looks suspicious too." Taking a sardine from another plate, he tilted his head back and swallowed it whole.

I tried to keep the anger from my voice because I had to play at being a servant. "Now you've had your little fun, so why don't you be good sports and let us get on with our work?"

The first guard studied me for a moment. "In a moment." He insolently raised the lid of another plate, and instantly the dungeon was filled with that light, sweet scent of Ebony's tears.

"What's this?" The second guard snatched the lid from the other and saw the number. "That's Monkey's cell. Since when has he been on a special diet?"

"Since today." Indigo snatched the flower from the plate. "He's got a tender stomach."

"No one's told us." The first guard grabbed her wrist in one paw and squeezed.

Indigo writhed. "Ow." Her claws loosened and the guard snatched the stalk of flowers from her hand.

"Please," Thorn begged, "we'll bring you our own meals as well as yours if you just leave us alone."

"But that's *hours* away." The first guard let the flower dangle languidly from one paw.

"I'll go back for them," Thorn offered.

"But I've a taste for something special." We watched horrified as the guard raised the stalk and bit off the top blooms. He chewed them thoughtfully and then grunted. "Nice—though it could use a bit more salt."

The second reached up to take the first guard's paw and forced him to lower the flower. "Let me see."

"No." Thorn sprang toward the second guard, but the first cuffed him so that he staggered back against the wall.

"You're in our dungeon now," the first dragon warned. "So don't tell us what to do. Or you could wind up in our care with all the other rotten scum." He held the last of the stalk out to the second guard.

The second guard leaned forward, clamped his lips around the stalk and, keeping his eyes on us, sucked the last flowers slowly into his mouth.

I let myself sag against the wall against which

Thorn already lay. All that sacrifice—just to put something into the stomachs of two piggish guards. It seemed that our clan and myself were fated to lose whatever we valued. I watched absently as the two laughing guards sampled more plates.

"Well"—the first guard picked his teeth with one dirty claw—"that wasn't bad for a snack."

The second guard settled back contentedly by the door. "Why didn't we think of doing this sooner?"

"It's never too late." The first guard waved us on airily. "Well, what are you staring at? Don't hang around here chatting. Go on."

Indigo didn't wait for another invitation but immediately began trundling the cart down to the first corridor of cells. Thorn and I, for want of something better to do, followed along behind her. While Indigo served the first cells, I tried to invent excuses that I could give to the sergeant and Lady Francolin; but I couldn't come up with any. I'd failed right when the clan had most needed and trusted me. Thrush was right: I was worthless.

It wasn't until we were out of sight of the guards that Indigo stopped the cart. "Why the long face?" she whispered.

I moped along. "I didn't exactly come here to visit Monkey."

Indigo opened the lower claws of one paw to reveal one delicate spray of blooms. "I don't know if this is enough, but I managed to snap off this much when I was holding the flower."

I snatched it from her paw. "It'll have to do." I was willing to grasp at any hope right now.

Thorn poked me in the side. "Let's go right to Monkey's cell."

"Not until we feed the other prisoners." Indigo took a plate from the cart. "Unless you want to hear enough bellowing and screeching to knock the palace down—and maybe make those two fools suspicious."

"She's right," I sighed. Wrapping my claws carefully around the flower, I followed Indigo and Thorn through the dungeon as they fed the prisoners and retrieved the plates from the last meal.

It seemed to take forever before we finally reached Monkey's cell once again. "Monkey," I called softly, "it's us."

Chains clinked as Monkey got off his bench and shuffled toward the door. "Who's that?"

"Who else would be visiting you? We brought

you the flower." I held the spray of flowers up triumphantly.

"Unh . . . good." Monkey stretched out his paw toward the door. "Thank you."

Something was wrong with the way Monkey was standing with those stooped, uncertain shoulders. I snatched the spray of flowers back just out of reach. This was the last, after all. "First, tell me what you're going to use them for."

Monkey wriggled his fingers at me. "I'll make magic."

I narrowed my eyes suspiciously. "How? I thought you had that needle in you."

"I'll show you." And his lips were already squirming as if he were muttering a spell.

I didn't wait for any more but thrust the flower spray into Thorn's startled paw and then touched my forehead myself. I'd had some experience making quick changes in shape and size so I was just a moment faster than the creature within the cell. I shrank down to about a tenth of a meter and shot through the opening.

Monkey was starting to lengthen out in the cell and his hair was hardening into scales. I wriggled and kicked determinedly. The trouble with shrinking down to such a small size is that it makes a meter into the equivalent of a kilometer.

"I knew you'd come back." The Grand Mage was already reaching for a ring of keys attached to his sash as I got to his eyes. Despite the wounds in my wings, I raised them and, with an extra hard flap, went sailing straight toward the right eyeball of the Grand Mage. "What?" He tried to jerk back his head, but I hooked my hind claws into his leathery eyelid and raised my forepaws over his pupil.

"Raise a paw or even wink that eye," I warned him, "and I'll take it out." And I bared my fangs for good measure. "And then I'll take out the other eye before you can even scream."

"How—how did you know that I wasn't the real Monkey?" the Grand Mage wondered.

"The real Monkey would have spent several minutes bragging about the magic he was going to do." I dug my claws in even tighter so he would know who was boss. "Now where is he?"

"Five—five cells down," the Grand Mage qua-vered. I could feel the trembling in his head as he tried not to move a muscle in his face. "Please, please, I'll do anything just so long as you don't blind me."

"Good," I grunted. "Go to the door." The cell

seemed to bob all around me as the Grand Mage obeyed. "Now open it." The Grand Mage still had the ring of keys in his paw. "Slowly," I warned.

"Yes, of course," the quivering Grand Mage said, and, putting the right key into the lock, turned it with a click.

Indigo and Thorn slipped into the cell the next moment and wound the Grand Mage's sash around his mouth so that he couldn't mutter spells. Then, leaving them to hold his paws flat against the floor so he couldn't sign any magic, I changed myself to my proper shape.

The Grand Mage's eyes widened when he saw me, and I could see him doing quick calculations as to what my plans might be. "I think you need a rest," I said. Snatching the ring of keys from his paw, I struck his temple with it and he pitched forward unconscious.

CHAPTER SIXTEEN

There was a furry creature five cells down, just as the Grand Mage had said. Short chains had him spread-eagled across the wall and a gag kept him from talking. "Well," I said as I began to try out the keys on the ring, "for once you can't talk back to me."

Though Monkey couldn't say anything, he wriggled his eyebrows eloquently at me and glared fiercely. I couldn't help chuckling. "That's a bit more like the Monkey that I know."

Thorn held up the spray of flowers. "We'd better be careful this time."

"Ask if he remembers the Green Darkness," Indigo suggested.

"One thing at a time." I jerked the door open as soon as I heard the key click in the lock.

Monkey wriggled his head and made loud muttering noises through the gag. "Well," I said as I crossed the cell warily, "since some dragons have the bad taste to want to try out fur, supposing you tell me a few things about yourself before we actually free you." And I took away his gag.

A torrent of words rushed from the frustrated ape. "Why, you overgrown lizard. How dare you make fun of the Master of the Seventy-Two Transformations?"

"None of which you can use at the moment," I felt obliged to point out; but I twisted around to grin at Thorn. "Now doesn't that sound like the authentic Monkey? He's the only ape proud enough to think of his dignity before his freedom."

Monkey dipped his head apologetically. "Well, this is hard treatment for a wizard who can climb through the clouds and stretch demons into toothpicks."

As I fitted the key back into the manacle around his left wrist, I held up the spray of flowers. "It was hard getting this for you; but we did."

Monkey frowned. "Is that all you could find?"

The first manacle fell away and I put the key into the manacle around his right wrist. "You don't know what this cost me and my clan."

When the second manacle had dropped, Monkey began to rub his wrists. "I'm sorry. It's just that . . ." He shook his head with a sigh. "Well, I was hoping for something of a reasonable size—not those tiny little things."

"I was hoping that you could save one flower from the spray." I bent to work on the manacles around his ankles. "It's the last of a very special type that used to bloom by the Inland Sea."

"I'm going to have to destroy it all. And just hope that one spray of flowers will be enough." As the manacles clanked against the wall, Monkey stamped his feet to restore the circulation there.

"I see." I stood up and took the flower from Thorn. "And you're sure the Lord of Flowers will help?"

Monkey paused in mid-stomp. "No."

I looked at him accusingly. "But you sounded so positive before."

Monkey massaged his left leg guiltily. "It's a bad habit of mine."

I twirled the spray of flowers thoughtfully between my claws, watching the tiny white flowers whirl around like dust motes in a wind. "It would still be possible to return this to the clan."

Indigo folded her arms over her chest. "Since when have you started to play it safe?"

I held the flowers beneath my snout so I could take in the soft, faint scent. "But I've got responsibilities now."

Indigo waved her hand around the cell. "They're trusting you to get them away from this kind of trap—not return their flower. I don't know who this Lord of Flowers is, but he sounds pretty powerful. Maybe he's just the sort of ally you need."

I pointed the flowers toward Thorn. "You're usually the first one who wants to give me advice. What do you think?"

Thorn tugged at his ear uncertainly. "If he says no, we can still carry out our original escape plan." He glanced at Indigo. "I hate to agree with her, but I think she's right. We didn't capture Civet by being cautious."

I guess that I'm a gambler by instinct. And my forehead tingled as if the dream pearl were agreeing with me. Impulsively, I held the flowers out to Monkey. "We're playing for high stakes now."

Monkey accepted the spray of flowers with a grave nod of his head. "I'll do my best, but maybe you three ought to leave the cell."

"Why?" Indigo demanded suspiciously.

Monkey held the flowers up to a dim patch of coral as if to admire it. "The Lord of the Flowers is a little . . . well, touchy about his privacy. He might not like my disturbing him."

I closed my eyes for a moment and sighed. I certainly would have had second thoughts about asking for the flower if I'd known that. "What else haven't you told us?"

"I think that's about it." Monkey used his free hand to shoo us from the cell. "You can watch from the doorway, though."

"That's kind of you," I said sarcastically as I took up a position there. Thorn and Indigo crowded in on either side.

Monkey knelt and began bowing toward one wall as he muttered a spell. The last spray of Ebony's tears rested on his open palms. Suddenly he bowed low from the waist, touching his forehead to the ground, and when he straightened up again, he clapped his palms together, crushing the spray of flowers.

I couldn't help wincing; and Thorn patted my shoulder sympathetically. "It's for the good of your clan," he murmured.

But I could only watch helplessly as Monkey

began to rub his palms against one another while he went on muttering the same droning spell. And—as if the last spray wanted to end with a certain style—the cell was filled with the scent of Ebony's tears.

Monkey stopped as he reached the end of the spell and looked frantically about the cell as if searching for something. Disappointed, he dropped his eyes wearily down to his palms as if he were trying to see if there was enough to go on with the magic.

"What's wrong?" I asked from the doorway.

But Monkey ignored me and, bowing his head, began to work the spell again. He rubbed his palms together more carefully this time, as if he had to preserve whatever petals were there. And, slowly, hesitantly, the light in the room began to change to a soft white and a mist seemed to fill it.

"Is it working?" Thorn nudged me.

"Who knows?" I shook my head.

Indigo clutched at my shoulder. "Look." But she didn't have to point; I could see it too, or I thought I did. I blinked my eyes once to be sure, but it was still there.

It was like a hole in the air—not a black spot

blocking our view of the far wall, but a hole behind which a gray cloud swirled and eddied. And the edges of the hole looked as if they had been drawn with a pen of blue light. Even as we watched, the scented mist shot into the hole as if there were someone on the other side sucking up the smoke.

Suddenly, we could hear the tramping of paws in the distance. "It must be a guard detail to check up on the Grand Mage." I shoved Thorn and then Indigo into the cell. It didn't seem to break Monkey's concentration at all as he went on working his spell. "Don't shut the door all the way," I said as I took the ring of keys from the door.

"What are you going to do?" Thorn asked in alarm.

"Buy time for Monkey." I jingled the keys at them.

Indigo stared at me in open puzzlement. "But you could be trapped, or even killed."

"It's time that I started living up to my clan's expectations." I darted down the corridor to Monkey's old cell and shut the door. The dragons sounded closer now. I didn't have much time to waste on wrong spells. Touching my forehead, I worked some signs and murmured the spell that would change me into the Grand Mage. Even as I felt my hide rippling and changing, I cast a spell on the Grand Mage that would transform him into my shape.

The dragons were in the corridor. "Here's the food cart, but not a sign of anyone," said a familiar voice. It was our old friend, the lieutenant.

"In here, hurry," I called.

The lieutenant poked his snout against the view slit in the door. "Sir?"

I pretended to adjust my fake sash. "I captured the outlaw."

"There were two others with her," the lieutenant said.

"What?" I swam to the door. "Quick. Go to the dungeon doors and don't let anyone out."

"But what about the outlaw's bearl, sir?" the lieutenant asked.

"I've got it already." I fitted the key into the lock; but to my chagrin, it was the wrong one.

The lieutenant watched as I tried another key. "Then it really doesn't matter when we catch them."

I put a third key into the lock. "We can't have them wandering around loose."

When that key didn't work, the lieutenant

squinted his eyes suspiciously. "Having trouble, sir?"

"It's just that there are so many keys." The fourth key did the trick.

The lieutenant stepped back doubtfully as I opened the door. "With all due respect, sir, I think His Most Exalted Majesty would like to have the bearl first." He signed to his squad. "Guard, escort His Wisdom."

Steel-tipped claws reached out toward me and I regretted that the Grand Mage didn't have the same. I would have to make do with my ordinary claws. Now I wasn't fighting just for me, but for my people. It was a new, unusual feeling, and I felt it help me throw off my cares and doubts just like a serpent shedding its old skin. I got ready to swipe at the guard on my right when a hound's shrill cry echoed down the corridor. Stunned, the guards just stood there with outstretched paws.

CHAPTER SEVENTEEN

A second hound barked and then a third and a fourth. I burst past the startled guards and barreled straight into the lieutenant. A quick shoulder sent him against the wall and then I was rushing down the corridor toward Monkey's new cell.

When I jerked the door open, Indigo seemed surprised to see me. "You're still alive. That was the noblest thing I've ever seen anyone do."

"Every now and then I manage to do things right." By the time I got to the cell door, a pack of hunting hounds filled the little room. Lean and sleek, with narrow flanks and waists, they seemed to be all chest and shoulder. Narrow muzzles were open to reveal sharp fangs, and their eyes searched the room intently as they milled about, puzzled by the narrow confines of the cell.

Monkey knelt in the very center. His arms were

held out from his sides and his palms turned upward with the fingers touching his thumbs. The hole in front of him had widened until it was some two meters high and three meters across so that it almost hid the wall behind it. "Let me do the talking," he warned us. "The Lord's whimsical at best; and downright dangerous at his worst."

A hunting horn sounded a long, low note that wound upward like a vine curling around a tree branch, and the pack surged back into the hole and out of the cell.

"What's going on?" The lieutenant shoved into the doorway.

I placed myself between him and the children. "Stay where you are. We've called up a magic older than the dragons; and it has whims and rules of its own."

Hooves clopped in the distance and a light began to fill the room. It grew brighter and brighter until we were all squinting. Even so, I could barely make out the silhouettes of riders on horses as they galloped up to the hole. And on their gauntleted wrists, they held hooded falcons.

"What happened to their heads?" Thorn gasped. "They look like flowers."

"Shush," I warned him. "Those are helmets."

But they were shaped cunningly like flowers—each different from the others: roses and lilies and peonies and birds of paradise. Their riding clothes, though of bright colors and a stylish cut, were of leather.

In contrast, though, the leader was short and squat with an ugly, pumpkin-shaped head, and he wore a suit sewn out of green leather cut in the shape of leaves so that he seemed to be wearing a bush. "Who dares disturb my riding?" he demanded impatiently as if he were ready to trample the culprit under his horse's hooves.

His horse pranced with a light, excited step up to the edge of the blue hole. And when the rider saw Monkey, his thick eyebrows drew together as if he were puzzled and disgusted all at once. Raising one gauntleted hand dramatically, he planted it on his hip. "I thought that of all people *you* would be the last to summon me."

Monkey rose and wiped at the slime on his knees as if to hide his own embarrassment. "So did I, Lord."

The Lord loosed the hood of his falcon. "Go, my beauty." And he launched the falcon with a quick motion of his hand. It flew straight into the cell and quickly circled as if there were no water but only clean air there.

Monkey did not move at all, but I couldn't help ducking as it flew through the doorway. With a startled yell, the lieutenant tumbled backward into the corridor. Hurriedly, I kicked the door shut with my hind leg.

The thick door didn't seem to bother the falcon at all. A small hole of blue light appeared on the door's surface as the falcon returned to the cell where it settled on his master's shoulder. The two stared intently at one another and then with a grunt, the man kicked his feet free of the stirrups and jumped down.

His legs were bowed as if centuries of riding had twisted them to the shape of his horse; and he had to waddle up to the hole to look into the cell. But he didn't break step as he walked into the water-filled room—as if he were used to that sort of thing. His felt boots with their leather soles slapped against the stones. "If this is one of your jokes, you'll be sorry." The Lord pulled off one gauntlet and felt the surrounding sea water curiously. "I tamed you once for your master. I can do it again."

"Now that was quite a chase," Monkey laughed, "and quite a battle."

The Lord of Flowers wriggled his potato-shaped nose as if—despite his best intentions—he was amused by the little ape. "I always catch the quarry I scent. But I don't think you called me to remember old hunts."

Monkey dropped his hand and bowed his head more seriously than I'd ever seen. "No, Lord. We have great need of your help."

"We?" He was intrigued in spite of himself. "Does this include all the dragons?"

Monkey turned and quickly pointed to Thorn, Indigo and myself. "No, just these three, Lord."

The Lord of Flowers squinted as if he were having trouble seeing us though we were only a meter away. "Then take your true shapes." He drew his gauntlet lightly over Thorn's head and his shape began to blur even as the Lord slipped the gauntlet over Indigo and myself.

When I had resumed my true shape, I heard the lieutenant take in a mouthful of water with a hiss. "It's the outlaw. Open up in the name of His Most Exalted Majesty." And then he stopped to shout to his squad. "Get reinforcements and a battering ram."

The Lord tugged his gauntlet back on and pointed at the door. "Don't you know it's rude to interrupt someone else's conversation?"

I peeked out through the view slit and saw that the stone of the corridor had turned to a mushlike material into which the lieutenant and his squad were sinking. And, of course, they made even more commotion than before. "I wouldn't shout like that," I warned, "or he might let you sink in all the way."

With a frightened look at the floor of the corridor, the lieutenant held up a paw to his squad. "Quiet now. Quiet. Do as Her Highness says." The title came readily to his lips now that he was in trouble.

First Indigo and then Thorn took a peek through the view slit. When Thorn looked away, he asked, "How did he do that?"

The Lord of Flowers rocked back a step as if he had just been struck a blow. "Just what sort of magic do they teach in school nowadays?"

Monkey held up a cautionary paw for us not to say anything more and then bowed back to the

Lord. "I gather that they don't teach magic any-more."

The Lord placed an astonished hand over his heart. "Nor heard of me?"

Monkey chose his words carefully. "It's what comes of staying out of the world, Lord."

The Lord lifted a gauntleted hand dramatically so Thorn could see. "Then listen well, boy. These gauntlets give me the power to turn anything back into their original elements and then into the shape I want."

When I nudged Thorn, he bowed his head. "I'm sorry that I didn't know you, Lord."

"Yes, well." The Lord brushed a hand over the leaves of his suit as if they were ruffled feathers. "See that you look up your local bard when you get home and find out all about me." Feeling slightly better, the Lord surveyed the room. "But where did you get flowers from the Inland Sea? I haven't smelled that delicious scent in ages."

Monkey nodded for me to go ahead so I spoke quickly, afraid of losing this vain creature's atten-tion. "They were the last, Lord. My clan has cher-ished them all these years, but I sent them to you in our need." I added as an extra bit of flattery for that proud lord. "Only you were worthy of them."

The Lord pressed his fingers beneath his throat as if that would help him clear it. "Harumph. That must be a very great need indeed."

"It is." And quickly I outlined the loss of the Inland Sea and my pursuit of Civet and our subsequent adventures here.

The Lord was tapping his foot impatiently before I finished. Apparently, he had very little interest in anything that didn't relate to him. "A very interesting tale, but what is that to me?"

Thorn started to get to his feet in his excitement. "Couldn't you restore the sea?"

"Hush." I pulled Thorn back down on his knees; but it was already too late.

The Lord squatted abruptly as if he couldn't quite believe his ears. "See here, boy. Even if they neglect elementary magic in your school, they still must teach manners."

Thorn sat back on his heels. "I didn't go."

The Lord sniffed. "Believe me. It shows."

Thorn spread his arms helplessly. "But I bet you could if you had some pity."

With a spinning jump, the Lord rose like a top out of control, and he threw back his head and laughed. "What does pity mean when you've lived as long as I have? Creatures come, creatures go; but the earth remains and my magic comes from the earth. I woke to the songs of creation. I will fall asleep to the songs of destruction."

Monkey watched intently, ready to stop the moment the Lord took offense. "Then perhaps you'd take us away from this palace to the mainland—if the Lord wouldn't mind."

The Lord irritably fiddled with his leafy collar. "I'm afraid that it's quite out of the question."

Monkey held up his hands hastily to show that he meant no insult. "But Lord—"

The Lord wagged his palm against the water as if he were already wiping Monkey's words away. "No, no. I've my reputation to think of, after all. I can't have my hunting interrupted by people asking for lifts. I tell you what I'll do. I'll give you the names of a half-dozen spirits who like doing all sorts of good deeds."

Appeals to his sense of pity didn't work so I decided to try working on his sense of humor.

"There may be other escorts, but none of them would be quite as colorful." Holding my breath, I shoved Thorn away from me in case this whimsical lord took it in his head to punish me.

But to my relief, he merely chuckled. "Colorful, is it?" The Lord whirled around and called through the hole toward his court. "Do you hear that? A name that was once dreaded around the world now belongs only to a colorful character."

As the Lord's court laughed politely, I added quickly, "But people would hear it often when the story gets told among dragons and humans."

The Lord held a thumb a few centimeters apart from his index finger. "And that is to be my gratuity—a little footnote to your story?"

Monkey clasped his hands behind his back. "The footnote could be longer if you'd help us get a few belongings that the High King stole. They'd be in his treasure vault."

The Lord threw back his head and let out a loud laugh. "Yes, very well, I suppose it's a small price to pay for such a large share of fame."

"Thank you, Lord." Monkey bowed his head and then gave me the thumbs-up sign.

"In the meantime, permit me." The Lord lifted

his gauntleted hand toward the needle in Monkey's chest and touched the tip. Blue electric sparks flew up and down the golden needle but neither Monkey nor the Lord seemed to feel anything; and the next moment the golden needle dissolved in the water as if it were merely cardboard.

There was no blood on Monkey's robe. In fact, there was only a small tear to indicate the needle had ever been there. Monkey looked down at his chest and then did a little pirouette. "Free. Free at last."

"A simple thank you would have sufficed." The Lord set one foot through the hole and the hounds, off in some unseen spot, began to bark happily.

"Hurry," Monkey beckoned to us, "before he changes his mind."

"What about the lieutenant and his squad?" Thorn wondered.

"The mages will take care of them." I slid one foreleg around Thorn and the other around Indigo. "Come along. Don't dawdle. The Lord's feeling kindly, but let's not depend on that too much." I felt each of the children place a hand on me in gratitude. We paused on the threshold of the hole. The riders sat patiently in the gray, swirling mist while the Lord of Flowers strode toward them.

"I don't see the ground there," Thorn gasped.

"The space between worlds doesn't have any ground," I said, and pulled them across.

CHAPTER EIGHTEEN

I felt a slight tingling as we crossed the threshold, but no pain. In fact, it was almost the opposite kind of feeling: I felt strangely alive—as if every cell in my body were finally waking up. I used to feel it some mornings when the rain had washed all the dirt from the air and everything looked so alive and new: The colors of the world seemed brighter, the sky a deeper blue, and everything was sharply outlined.

And yet there were no solids, let alone colors, around us. I found myself walking over the mist. It had a little give like the spongey floor of an old forest, but it supported our weight safely.

A dozen men and women sat waiting for us. Their silk tunics and trousers were of a soft pastel green, but their felt vests were colored bright red and gold and blue. And the horse's elaborate head-dresses matched those of their riders.

Each of them had some weapon too—some, great curving bows made of horn. Others had cross-bows. Still others had spears about two meters long with thick shafts and metal tines projecting at right angles.

The Lord gestured to Monkey. "I daresay you know this fellow."

There was good-natured laughing from the riders. "He gave us the best hunt of all—once," a woman nodded. Her helmet was shaped full of sprays of little yellow flowers that gave it a fuzzy look.

"And never again if I can help it." Monkey doffed his hat and bowed to them all. "Your hounds worried fur off in a dozen places."

"And these are his friends." The Lord turned and waved vaguely toward us. "I don't believe I got their names."

I cleared my throat awkwardly. "I am Her Highness, Princess Shimmer, of the . . ." I debated on whether to use "Lost Sea" or "Inland Sea" and decided to be more positive about the future. "The Inland Sea." The children still had hold of me and I nodded first to Thorn. "This is Thorn." And I indicated Indigo. "And Indigo."

The Lord of Flowers vaulted into the saddle of his horse. He looked much taller and finer as he sat upright on his horse—as if that were his natural place. "Right. Now that the pleasantries are over. Let's be off to the High King's treasure vaults." The Lord let out a whistle and the well-trained hounds leapt up on the saddle pommels where they perched as easily as if they were sitting on the ground. "I can smell the magic this way." And, turning his horse's head, he began to trot off to his left.

"Quick." I hoisted Thorn up on my back and then Indigo.

"Ow," Thorn complained to Indigo. "Don't squeeze my waist so hard."

I began to trot after the Lord. "Don't quarrel, or you'll both have to run." I stole a glance behind us toward the hole, which was slowly shriveling shut.

Monkey fell in pace beside me. "They thought they had old Monkey; but they ought to know no dungeon can hold me."

I frowned at the boastful little ape. "You had a little help as I recall."

Monkey grinned. "Are you hinting that you'd like a thank you?"

"No," I grunted. "I'd hate to strain your self-composure."

Monkey clasped his paws together. "You've got a friend for life."

Having a friend like the unpredictable Monkey was almost as bad as holding a sword by its edge. You could never be sure when you were going to be cut. "That's not what I was asking for either."

"Too late." Monkey shrugged. "You're stuck with me now. Once I like someone, I never give up on them."

"Wonderful," I muttered. "That's just what I needed on top of everything else. A personal curse."

But Monkey was as good as his word. He refused to take offense but only chuckled. "You do have a spiny sense of humor, though."

We had to hurry a little then to keep sight of the Lord of Flowers. The mist hissed as the horses' hooves crushed it and yet they clopped against something hard—as if the mist were more solid farther on down. The clouds swirled all around us, sometimes taking the shape of a wall and once the face of a startled dragon, but most of the time it was a world without shape or form. But the

Lord of Flowers seemed sure of himself. Every now and then he would stop and sniff the air and then he would point us in a different direction.

"This is it," he finally announced, and brought us to a halt. Flinging up his free hand, he murmured something, and a bright blue point of light appeared in the cloud. And it was as if someone had dropped a coal on a piece of paper. The blue light seemed to eat at the mist as the hole widened.

Monkey and I slipped past the patient riders to the hole and looked into a vast, shadowy room that was lit only here and there by patches of coral. Shelves filled with treasure chests and gold vessels seemed to stretch on for two hundred meters into the distance and fifty meters on either side. The ceiling itself was lost somewhere in the shadows after twenty meters.

"Where are the guards?" Thorn whispered cautiously.

I studied the vault but I didn't see anyone. "They'd probably be outside, and they'd need a mage or someone with a bit of magic to open the doors themselves."

Monkey's fingers twitched. "If I weren't reformed, what couldn't I take from here."

The Lord's horse stamped its hooves and he had

to bring it back under control. "What are you waiting for? I don't intend to stay here indefinitely. I'll count to a thousand, and after that the hole will close."

Monkey glanced at the Lord and then rolled his eyes at me. This was one order, it seemed, that must be obeyed. "It sounds like we'd better hurry then." And he hopped through the hole.

"Wait for me." And I sprang after him.

I felt that same faint twinge when I crossed the threshold of the hole, but this time it felt as if my hide were growing duller and older once again— as if I'd left behind whatever renewing effect the mists had.

"Look at this." Monkey held up two gold vases that were identical. Behind him, I could see another dozen more like it.

"That's a little extravagant even for Sambar," I said, and then I saw that there were dozens of the same objects. "He's made duplicates."

Monkey threw the vases back on the shelf in disgust. They made a loud bonging sound. "Good luck picking out the real one."

"You have to give us more time," Thorn called to the blue hole.

"Seventy-nine," was the Lord's answer.

"This calls for magic—and a lot of it." Monkey began stripping the hairs from his tail until he had two handfuls. Then, spitting on them, he threw them up in the water. "Change!"

And instantly the water was filled with clouds of little monkeys who were getting tangled up in everything.

I swatted a couple away from my mouth. "And I thought one of him was too much."

But Monkey just laughed and clapped his hands. "Children, children, go find old Monkey's little needle now."

Thorn plucked at his sleeve. "And Baldy's cauldron."

"And the cauldron." Monkey looked at me to elaborate on that description.

I held my hands in a shape about the size of my head. "It's made of bronze and has a face on each side."

Monkey flapped his paws as if he were chasing away clouds of mosquitoes instead of little duplicates of himself. "You heard her. Now go off—and be quick about it." And the little monkeys scattered across the room.

"We'd better look ourselves." I began to trot

down an aisle past shelves of mirrors and magical bowls of gold and crystal, but nothing that looked like the magical cauldron I wanted.

Behind me, I could hear Indigo keeping a worried count. She was up to three hundred when we found Civet laid out on the lower shelf of one aisle. She was still dressed in the long dress and pleated jacket she had been wearing when we had brought her to the palace; but her turban of gold cloth and all her jewelry had been taken away.

"Now why would they put her here?" Thorn wondered.

"You ought to know Sambar by now. He hates to let anything magical slip out of his grasp." I went over to her and poked one leg. The flesh felt firm enough. "She knows a good deal of magic so if the mages couldn't break Monkey's spell, they probably cast a light sleep spell over her and stowed her away here." I twisted my head around to look at my back. "Do you think you can keep her on my back?"

"You're going to take her with us?" Indigo looked at her doubtfully.

I slid her sleeping form from the shelf. "Maybe we can wake her up and strike a bargain: her help in exchange for Monkey's removing the chain."

"Well, at least there's only one of her." Thorn took her arms and helped slide her onto my back. "How are we going to carry the cauldron and all its duplicates?"

"I don't know." I trotted grimly down the next aisle. "But somehow I keep thinking that there has to be a simple way to tell which is the real one." I looked around the treasure vault. "And it's got to be in the vault itself or fetching anything from here would take forever."

"Three hundred and seventy-five," Indigo said.

"Your Highness, Your Highness." An excited little duplicate of Monkey came somersaulting through the water. "We found the cauldron."

"Show me," I said, "and hurry." It didn't take me long to regret that I'd said it because that little monkey took me literally at my word. As small as he was, he somersaulted through the water so that I had to race to keep up with him. Twice I skidded and went into shelves instead of turning a corner.

We passed by a perplexed Monkey who was sorting through a tub of needles. He would hold one up and shout "Change" and when nothing would happen, he would discard it on the floor.

At the same time, several dozen other monkeys on the rim of the tub were helping him so that Monkey was already ankle deep in iron needles.

My legs almost buckled when we finally got to the right aisle. A dozen monkeys leapt up and down. "Here they are. Here they are."

There were nearly a hundred bronze cauldrons. Each was shaped like a rectangle with ornate legs and faces carved into the sides—one of the unicorn, another of the phoenix, a third of a dragon, and a fourth of a turtle.

"Sambar certainly isn't taking any chances on someone finding the right cauldron," I said in dismay. "This would take several days."

"Four hundred and fifty," Indigo counted.

"And we don't even know a test to pick out the right one," Thorn said. He leaned over from my back to touch the face on one cauldron.

I felt the guardian before I heard or saw him. There was a vibration beneath my paws as if the stone were beginning to bubble; and then I heard the scrabbling noise of claws. "Let go of the cauldron," I ordered and sprang back. "I knew that this was too easy."

The stone floor began to crumble on the spot

where we had stood. And suddenly a long-haired creature thrust its head up. Its skull was shaped like a melon surrounded by golden wires and its eyes were glowing red that seemed all the redder against the pale white flesh of its face. Tusks like a boar's sprang from either corner of its mouth. It began to squirm.

"Quick," Thorn said, "before it gets its arms free."

However, I was already taking a swipe at the head; but I was too late. A club with huge spikes broke through the stone floor and blocked my blow. And with a huge twist and wriggle, it appeared up to its waist and suddenly I was facing six arms, each with a weapon. In its upper left, it had the club, but it was also armed with an axe, a mace, a short sword, a sickle as well as a small shield.

"I think this calls for a strategic retreat." I began to swim frantically away from it while the little monkeys tumbled through the water shouting the alarm.

Monkey, however, refused to leave the tub of needles. "I'm not leaving my magic rod behind. I feel naked without it."

"It's better than having no head at all," I snapped.

I felt the same funny vibrations that I had felt before. I moved back just as the guardian popped up out of the floor and seized Monkey by the ankles. It was almost as if it could move through stone the way a mole could move through dirt.

"Five hundred and one," Indigo announced.

I was beginning to be sorry that the child had ever learned how to count.

CHAPTER NINETEEN

There wasn't time for Monkey to make a horde of larger apes to help him. He was too busy trying to keep the guardian from tearing him in two. As the guardian clambered out of the hole, it held Monkey aloft between its two upper hands.

Monkey bent over and chopped his paws at the guardian's neck. With a howl, the guardian let go of him; but before Monkey could scramble to safety, it grabbed him in its middle pair of hands.

I bent forward on my forelegs. "Get off," I ordered the children. I didn't intend to get into a fight with them on my back.

"No," Monkey shouted, "find my rod for me." His words vibrated in a funny way because the guardian was pummeling him with its upper fists while the two lower pairs held his legs and waist in an unshakable grip.

All the other little monkeys had gathered by the tub and were frantically picking up needles and shouting "Change" and then discarding the needles in a regular rain when they didn't prove to be the right one.

"There has to be a way of finding the real one." I looked around desperately but I didn't see anything.

"Would it be a special magical word?" Thorn suggested.

"No," Indigo reasoned, "because that would affect everything in the room."

"Maybe there's some special magical object that the mages use to touch an object." I had to dart out of the way as Monkey and the struggling guardian upset a set of shelves and sent bowls and plates of paper-thin china crashing on the floor.

"That would still take time." Thorn drew a perplexed hand over his face. "And the mages might need the treasure in a hurry if there was some kind of emergency."

"So it has to be something that can find the treasure fast." I heard Indigo slap her legs in frustration. "But what?"

"It looked so small and ordinary at the time that I didn't think much about it," Thorn said slowly.

"But maybe it's like the island. It didn't look like much from the surface."

"What do you mean by 'it'?" Indigo wondered.

"It was a mirror," Thorn said thoughtfully, "and the strange thing was that there was only one of it."

"You may be brighter than you look," Indigo admitted grudgingly.

"I'm willing to try anything at this point." I started to trot down the aisle. "Where is it?"

"It was back in that section where all the other mirrors were." Thorn gripped my neck as a precaution as I hurried to the aisle of magical mirrors. There were all sorts of mirrors from gold ones as tall as a human to brass ones set in ornate frames of precious metals and jewels.

I slowed so we could look at the shelves carefully. "I don't see it."

"It's somewhere along here," Thorn muttered. "Like I said, it seemed so ordinary that I didn't really pay much attention to it."

We passed about thirty meters' worth of shelves filled with duplicates of precious or magical mirrors. From not too far away, we could follow the progress of the fight by the crash of breaking objects.

"Maybe we should think about getting Monkey and heading for the hole." Indigo's voice had risen an octave in her anxiety.

I was about to agree with Indigo when Thorn shouted, "Wait. There it is!"

I skidded to a halt and then whipped around and retraced my steps.

The object was so small that I hadn't seen it in the shadows made by a dozen golden hand-held mirrors. "What's this?" I peered at what seemed to be an antique circular brass mirror about a third of a meter in width. It had been turned face down so we could see the simple grain pattern on its back, and at the center of the back was a knob by which it could be held. Around the rim ran a motto: "Do not deceive."

"You said there were four symbols of dragon power," Thorn prompted me.

"Yes, bowl, mirror, cloud and pearl." I took the knob between my claws and turned the mirror over; but I was disappointed only to see my reflection and, behind me, the two curious children.

"Well, what does the dragon mirror look like?" Thorn almost fell over as he tried to stretch himself closer to examine the mirror.

"I don't know. I never saw it myself." I passed

the mirror back to them so they could inspect it themselves. "But if this was a magic mirror, don't you think they would have put it in a more ornate frame?"

"Not if they want to fool you." Thorn held it out to Indigo; but she shook her head.

Disappointed, Thorn held the mirror by its rim and wagged it in the air. "But there has to be some reason why this mirror is kept here when everything else looks so expensive."

"I don't know." Indigo reached her hand out to trace the motto and announced in a mock solemn tone, "But take its advice: Do not deceive yourself."

"There has to be something special about it." Thorn held it away from her pointing finger; and in so doing he held it so that I could see the mirror's front again.

"Hold it right there," I ordered, and twisted my neck around to look. Where there had been a dozen vanity mirrors, there was now only one reflected in the mirror; but when I looked at the shelves, I still saw a dozen of them. "This is it. We just needed to speak the spell that was written on the back." Raising a foreleg, I shoved the children upright and began to swim back toward the battling Monkey.

Despite all the little apes, there was still half a tub of needles to go through. But while we had been gone, Monkey and the guardian had managed to wreck most of the section. Broken stone shelves lay with crushed or dented or broken bowls and cups. However, in the meantime, Monkey had managed to get around behind the guardian's head and was trying to squeeze its thick neck with his legs while he clutched at its head with his paws.

"Save yourself," Monkey shouted to us. "I'll hold him as long as I can."

With a yowl, the guardian dropped to its knees and bent over so suddenly that Monkey went tumbling head over heels like a round, furry ball.

I charged over the debris. "Just keep the guardian away from us for another moment; and we'll have your magical rod for you."

"There's no problem about that." Monkey bounced to his feet and tried to leap to the top of another set of shelves, but the guardian whipped one of its hands around his paw. And then it began to squeeze so that Monkey shouted, "Children, come to me."

And all the little apes rose from the tub like a cloud of flies and began to buzz around the guardian; but though it used its five other hands to slap at the apes that pinched, bit and kicked it, the guardian did not let go of Monkey.

I thrust my forepaw behind me. "Give me the mirror."

"Here." Thorn set it between my claws and I held it above the tub.

"Do not deceive me," I murmured fervently, and I angled it so that I could see the tub reflected on the mirror's surface. I saw only one little iron needle that seemed to float halfway up the tub because the layers of fakes underneath it were now invisible.

I plunged my paw into the tub. It was a strange sensation to feel the iron needles without seeing them. It was like putting my hand into a barrel of cold iron nails. But as I moved my paw toward Monkey's needle, it moved away under the pressure of the fake ones. As a result it took me several attempts before I grasped the real needle.

"Here." I held the needle aloft.

A little ape snatched it from my claws and then somersaulted back to Monkey, who now had his head trapped under one of the guardian's arms despite all the little apes' attempts to distract it.

The guardian tried to catch the little ape in one of its hands, but the ape was too nimble for it and darted instead into Monkey's paw. "Change!" Monkey called triumphantly.

And the needle swelled in his hand until it was a rod of black iron about a third of a meter long. At either end was a golden loop. Quickly Monkey rammed a loop into the guardian's sides. The guardian gave a grunt and clutched the spot between a pair of its hands. Monkey hammered the short iron rod against the guardian's stomach and with a whoosh of expelled water, the guardian let go of Monkey and fell backward on a pile of broken china. It leapt up almost as quickly when it felt the sharp shards.

Monkey twirled the short rod in his hand and then smacked the tip against the palm of his other paw. He held it aloft. "Change!" And the rod grew to the length of two meters. The iron rod should have weighed several times what he did, but Monkey whirled it in a circle over his head as if it were only a bamboo stick. The guardian shrank back. "Go on," Monkey shouted. "Get your cauldron."

I hesitated. So many people were depending on me, but it wouldn't do them any good if I were caught right now. In the distance, I could hear shouting from the heavy doors to the vault. I suppose those would be the guards who had been alerted by all the commotion, but as yet they hadn't been able to open the magical doors. More importantly, it must be time for the Lord's blue hole to disappear.

"No, we'd better go back," I sighed. "A gambler has to know when she's taking too many chances."

Of all people, it was Indigo who protested. "You can't disappoint your people. The Lady gave up the flower. The sergeant and her squad may have given up their lives. Their sacrifices have to mean something."

"It can't be helped." I forced myself to shrug.

"But it isn't right." Indigo kicked a heel against my side. "Your clan is counting on you."

I sighed. "What's one more wrong added to a long list of sins?"

"Not if I have anything to say about it." Indigo jumped down from my back, and before I could stop her, she had snatched the mirror from my paw.

I twisted around, but she already was running down the aisle toward the cauldron. "But it's not your responsibility."

"Maybe everyone has the responsibility to end a wrong." She backed down the aisle almost cheerfully—as if she had finally begun to understand what Thorn and I had been saying. "Like you said: There's more to life than surviving."

Monkey slammed his rod so hard against the floor that the heavy stone cracked. As the guardian cringed in front of him, Monkey brought his staff down again only centimeters away. "Get your ugly face out of here," he shouted. And the guardian, nodding its head gratefully, began scrabbling with all six hands at the stone.

With his rod over his shoulder, Monkey held out his hand and four little apes settled on his palm. "Change," he said to them, and was quick to drop his hand away as they began to grow. "Go help the girl, children."

Thorn shook his head as he watched the apes, each now as large as Monkey himself, somersault down the aisle. "How do you like that? She was listening to us after all."

"I guess all those speeches were bound to sink

in." I was a little surprised—and ashamed—that Indigo was willing to risk more for my people than I was.

Thorn scratched behind his ear guiltily. "I guess there really is some hope for her."

"And maybe for all of us," I sighed.

Thorn lowered his hand. "Do you think they'll be in time?"

The guardian was almost out of sight now. Monkey deliberately tapped his rod against the floor again, and with a squeal, the guardian disappeared. "I don't know, but maybe we can convince the Lord of the Flowers to wait a moment longer."

"Let's just hope that the hole is still there." I began to swim as fast as I could considering my two awkward burdens. I didn't enjoy the prospect of sampling Sambar's hospitality a second time.

We hurried as fast as we could to the spot where the hole was. It had already shrunk to half its size, but we could still step through easily. The Lord was sitting impatiently on his horse. "It's about time. Now let's be off."

"Lord," Monkey gasped. "You have to give us time for the girl to get back."

The Lord stared at Civet, who lay draped over my back. "Good Heavens. Who's that?"

"A witch who can also help us." When Monkey murmured "Change" to his staff, it shrank to the size of a needle again, which he tucked behind one ear with an immensely self-satisfied air.

The Lord raised his hands in exasperation. "Anything else to bring? No elephants or unicorns?"

"No, Lord," Monkey said quickly, "the girl and the cauldron are the last things we need."

"You said you had a few belongings to fetch—not this menagerie." The Lord gripped the reins irritably. "Oh, very well. I'll stay till the hole closes. But then I'm leaving."

"Thank you, Lord." Monkey turned to the cloud of little monkeys and they began to whirl like a disk until their bodies blurred. Then the disk began to shrink as the bodies changed back into thin hairs; and they flew downward in a long, slender stream that began to cover Monkey's tail.

Suddenly in the distance we heard a shriek. "We shouldn't have left her," I said guiltily. I twisted a foreleg around and lowered Civet to the floor. "Monkey, will you see what you can do about restoring the sea? I made a promise to my people. Perhaps you can get Civet to cooperate."

"Don't worry." Monkey raised his hairy tail like a banner. "Now that Monkey is involved, there'll be no trouble."

It was Monkey's carelessness that had let Civet loose the waters of our sea on a helpless city; but since I was asking a favor of him, I didn't think I ought to point that out. "Thank you." I tried to unwrap Thorn's arms from around my neck. "Get off, boy."

"No." Thorn clung even tighter. "We're a team, remember?"

I tugged harder at his arms. "But you don't even like her."

"Not until she went after the cauldron," Thorn admitted. "I guess she really is more like you than I thought."

The doors to the vaults suddenly crashed open and a dozen dragons swept over the shelves. "I'm closing the doorway." The Lord began to raise his gauntleted hand.

"No, wait." Monkey peered intently through the shadowy vault. "I see my children coming."

One pair of apes was somersaulting through the

air with the cauldron between them. The other pair held a protesting Indigo. But it was hard for her to make her point since the angry words ended in a yelp every time the pair that was holding her did a somersault.

"There are the thieves," a dragon shouted; and six dragon guards shot into the air, as slim and deadly and swift as arrows.

Monkey cupped his hands around his mouth like a megaphone. "Hurry, children. Hurry."

Beside me, Thorn was clenching his fists. "Come on, come on," he encouraged them.

But as fast as the apes tumbled, the dragons swam faster. Two dragons split off at an angle to cut them off while the other dragons divided into two pairs to intercept both the cauldron and Indigo. The apes with the cauldron dropped it as they got ready to fight; and the treasure vault reverberated with the clonging sound—as if we were inside a bronze bell.

But after wanting the cauldron all this time, it suddenly didn't seem so important anymore. We would find a way somehow to restore the sea. But what really mattered was a courageous soul like Indigo's. It shouldn't go to waste in Sambar's dungeons. I realized that I had been wrong: It wasn't the dream, but the dreamer that was priceless. There was really only one thing for me to do.

Arching my back suddenly, I used my tail to knock Thorn into Monkey's startled arms. "Take care of him in case I don't get back."

"Hey!" Thorn struggled to break free.

Tensing my legs, I sprang through the hole. "Obey Monkey." Spreading my wings, though they still ached, I used them to send me plunging through the water.

The Lord raised his hand in warning. "The same applies to you. I leave as soon as the hole closes."

"Come back," Thorn shouted from below.

But I was already speeding toward the guards. "I can't let her do all the work. This is for *my* clan, after all."

CHAPTER TWENTY

I caught the first pair of guards by surprise. They slowed for a moment as if wondering what other thieves might be hiding in the vault. That moment of hesitation was all that I needed. Sounding the war cry of my clan, I charged right between them. I had no time for tournament rules. This was a brawl where I had to disable them as quickly as I could.

Whirling and lashing my tail, I struck out with my claws and beat at them with my wings. I felt a tearing pain in one of my wings—as if I had reopened one of my old wounds; but that couldn't be helped. I heard frightened cries and felt my tail strike a blow that vibrated all the way up my spine; and the bones of my wings ached as they struck hard skulls.

And then, with a wriggle of my whole body, I

was shooting on through the water. From the corners of my eyes, I could see one dragon sinking unconscious to the floor as the other was trying to swim away while she held her foreleg against her chest as if the leg were broken. Below me, I could hear Thorn and Monkey shouting their encouragement.

Just ahead of me were the first apes. "Get the cauldron and take it to the hole," I shouted, and they barely leapt out of my way as I swam past.

The next pair of dragons hit me at full speed with their fangs exposed and claws extended. But I was ready for them. Tucking my head and tail against my body, I made myself into a ball that dropped through water. They were moving so fast that they couldn't stop in time even when they spread out their wings. And they were so close that their wings beat against one another. The result was that they stopped in complete confusion.

I had tumbled over so that my back was to the floor. I straightened out my head and tail then and a kick of my legs sent me upward. A blow of my tail knocked out the first one, and she went falling toward the floor where she crashed among the mirrors. And I kept spinning in a full circle so that my tail smashed against the wings of the second. He just hung there in pain.

The third pair was led by my old friend, the lieutenant. "I've had enough of you," I growled.

"Thief." He dashed at me with outstretched claws; but I arched over his back between his wings. A moment later, my claws had opened a wound on his neck so that he dropped away, clutching it.

But by that time the other dragon had caught up with Indigo. "Stop," she shouted, "stop." And she reached a hand into her waistband and pulled out the mirror. "Come near me and I'll drop this and break it."

It was a bluff, of course, because a fall from that distance probably wouldn't even dent the mirror; but the Grand Mage, who was about twenty meters away, couldn't be sure of that.

"Listen to her," the Grand Mage ordered, and the guard veered away to the left.

"Your Wisdom," I called to him, "you know what will happen if she destroys the mirror." I swam quickly toward Indigo. "It will be chaos in the vault if you lose the mirror."

"It's one of the great treasures of the High King." Alarmed, the Grand Mage froze in the water. "Please don't do anything to it."

"At the moment, Uncle Sambar's feelings aren't my major concern." A final kick sent me sailing toward Indigo. The last guard was moving in a wide circle.

"But I can't let you take the cauldron," the Grand Mage quavered.

"I'm just going to borrow it for a little while. You have my word that I'll return it." Hooking a foreleg around Indigo's waist, I drew her onto my back.

She couldn't have been more surprised than if I had just told her she was my mother. "You could have escaped with the cauldron. Why did you come for me?"

I signed for the apes to begin moving toward the hole. I wasn't sure how big the hole was, but I knew we had to hurry if we were going to have any chance of making it. "You're not the only one who can be noble."

Indigo gave a little excited, skeptical laugh. "Me? Noble? I was only trying to help you keep your promise to your clan."

"And that makes you far more noble than a spoiled worm like Uncle Sambar." I held my left forepaw behind me. "Give me the mirror." As the guard closed to within meters of us, I held up the antique. "Your Wisdom, I swear that I'll crumple this in half if your guard gets in our way."

"Please." The Grand Mage clutched his paws together and added hastily, "Your Highness."

It was strange how a little fear could make him start using my proper title—just as it had done with the lieutenant. The guard looked to the Grand Mage for orders; and I decided to take advantage of her uncertainty. "Get out of my way," I commanded.

The guard hesitated for just a fraction of a second and I took the opportunity to dart over her.

"No, no." The Grand Mage flung up his paws frantically. "Don't let her escape."

But I was already drawing away. "Catch it before it breaks," I yelled, and spun the mirror out over the middle of the vault.

The guard plunged desperately after the mirror while I raced the two apes through the water. But when I first saw the hole at twenty meters, it only seemed to be a pinpoint of blue light.

"Hurry," Monkey shouted through it. Lowering my head and folding my wings over Indigo, I began to kick and wriggle for all I was worth.

Ten meters from the hole, I could see that it was really about a meter wide. Monkey had poked his head through the hole and was waving his hand at us frantically. "The Lord's already leaving."

I aimed myself like an arrow toward the hole. "Then get out of the way, idiot." Monkey jumped back as I shot toward the hole. "Jump when I tell you," I instructed Indigo. When I was only two meters away, I skidded to a halt. The hole had shrunk to only two-thirds of a meter now. There was no way I could fit through it in my present size. "Now," I shouted to Indigo and spread my wings to their fullest so that the extra surface dragged at the water and I came to an abrupt stop.

Indigo kicked off my back and through the hole and the two apes were right on her heels. Touching my forehead, I murmured the spell and worked the sign that would make me smaller.

Monkey's face appeared in front of the hole. It was barely large enough for his head now. His paws pulled at the hole's edges as if he could keep the hole from shrinking anymore. "Come on. Don't quit now."

My head snapped back against my spine and my bones ached as they began to grow short. I felt as if someone were hammering all my bones together to make them smaller and denser. Even so, I forced my body toward that hole. But the process of shrinking seemed to be taking forever. And worse: as I shrank, so did the hole.

I could only see the upper part of Monkey's face and his worried eyes watching me; but they seemed much larger now in comparison to my size—almost like the head of a giant. I kicked and swam with all my might toward the hole; but now that I was smaller once again, the distance was greater. I tried to swim toward the hole, but it might as well have been a thousand meters as well as a meter.

Still, my clan would know that I had tried to keep my promises. I think I had the right to call myself their princess now—whatever Uncle Sambar might do. But after this theft—I expected a session with his torturers and then a quick swim to the executioner's block.

Suddenly, Monkey's paw shot through the hole. His wrinkled palm seemed as broad as a field as it closed over me.

"Hey," I said. And then I was yanked through the water. I felt a brief tingling as I was pulled through the hole and then I was on the other side— and not a moment too soon. The hole made a soft sucking sound as it closed for good.

CHAPTER TWENTY-ONE

I suppose I should have been more grateful, but at the moment I didn't like being treated like someone's pet ferret. "Let me down," I ordered.

"I don't know," Monkey observed lazily. "I think this size is more suitable for you." He gave a shout when I bit his thumb, and suddenly I was flung into the gray mist that surrounded us. "Ow. That hurt." He waved his paw. "That's a dragon's gratitude for you."

I extended my wings and flapped them with difficulty. I was beginning to feel the pain from the reopened wounds. "And you'll get more of the same if you try that again. Just because you're bigger doesn't make you any smarter or better than me."

Indigo squatted down and examined the cauldron. "What happened? It's cracked now."

"It probably got that when it was dropped." Monkey was busy changing the last four apes to hairs and restoring them to his tail. "Don't worry. We can get it fixed."

Thorn cleared his throat. "And anyway, you got it. I owe you an apology for some of the things that I said about you." I think it was harder for him to apologize to Indigo than it had been to defy Uncle Sambar.

Indigo squirmed as if she were far more used to insults than to praise. "No, they were true enough."

Thorn was just as uncomfortable as she was. "But there was more to you than I was willing to admit. Shimmer saw it; but I was too stubborn."

Indigo rose with an awkward smile. She seemed willing to make her own peace with him. "I don't know if there was all that much there to begin with."

"*May* we leave now?" the Lord of Flowers asked sarcastically.

Indigo spun around on her heel. "How about dropping us off at the Green Darkness?" she asked expectantly.

Monkey clutched his head and I held my breath. We both expected the Lord to scold her or even punish her for being so forward. But she'd managed to catch his fancy. "Yes, that might be pleasant. I haven't seen that spot since . . ." He paused and plucked his lip. "Well, I can't remember. But," he added with a glance at Monkey, "I'm sure you weren't born yet to devil my days so the world must have been a good deal younger and calmer." He gestured to the rose-helmeted man. "Take the Witch. And Artemisia"—he pointed to the woman in the fuzzy, yellow helmet—"take Her Highness." He assigned another rider to take the cauldron and two more to take Thorn, Indigo and Monkey.

"If you just give me a moment, I can change myself back into my proper size and ride beside you." I started to reach a paw toward my forehead when I saw the Lord's face.

He was wriggling his nose and twitching his lips as if he were trying to hold something in. Finally, he gave up and let out a loud laugh. "Oh, you are a droll creature. The fastest dragon could never keep us with us."

Artemisia trotted over obligingly. "You can either

ride behind me, Your Highness, or on my shoulder." There was a hound still sitting in its place in front of her.

"On your shoulder," I said, and fluttered over to her vest and settled down. She gave off a warm, musty fragrance that reminded me of hot, sunlit summer afternoons.

"Sink your claws into my vest, Your Highness," she cautioned. "When the Lord really rides, there is nothing swifter."

The Lord circled, his horse stamping its hooves nervously as if it were eager to be off. "Are we all ready?" He looked around expectantly. When there was no answer, he wheeled his horse smartly. "Then let's ride." And he went galloping into the mist; and with shrill yelps the other riders followed him.

I quickly realized that I had made a mistake when I chose to ride on her shoulder. I wanted to close my eyes as the mist whipped past us, but I didn't dare while the others could see me.

We charged up one cloudy swell and down another and sometimes we bobbed up and down as her horse rode over the tops of what looked like billowing waves. At that reckless pace, I kept waiting for one of the horses to stumble; but none faltered. It was almost as if their hooves had eyes that always found sure footing.

I looked down at the mist as we passed and it seemed that the waves were forever changing. The walls of the palace dissipated into a shapeless mist that I guessed was this place's equivalent of open sea. But then the clouds swirled and seemed to rise up around us like high canyon walls and then collapse into meadowlands. And suddenly we were galloping down a street filled with strange beetle shapes that seemed to roll along as fast as the horses.

Artemisia was so intent upon following the Lord's breakneck pace that it took me a while to work up my nerve to ask her. "Where are we?"

Her answer was broken up by the rhythmic galloping of her mount. "In the place . . . between worlds . . . between the way things were . . . and are . . . and will be."

I suppose this was what the Lord meant by riding—not just a quick canter but darting through a universe of possibilities. It was small wonder that our own problems seemed petty to him. I began to understand just how much arrogance Monkey had when he had asked him for help. "And just what does he hunt?"

"Oh, monsters and ghouls . . . and wayward thieves . . . and mages," Artemisia said as casually as if she were talking about rabbits and foxes. "Whatever we're asked . . . to track down."

I couldn't help shuddering. "I wouldn't like to be his quarry."

"Then behave yourself." She winked.

Eventually, the mist seemed to settle down into what seemed like masses of land under a gray, metallic sky. Once I thought I recognized the shape of a set of undersea ridges, but then it swelled and spread outward into another shape. It was almost as if, in this mist-filled place, the world were shrinking underneath the horses' hooves; or we were growing—swelling to the size of giants who could cross an entire ocean in just a few strides. If this was part of the Lord's magic, he would be a very dangerous pursuer indeed.

Ahead of us, the air shone a bright blue like a frame of light hung on a wall of bright green glass. Without even hesitating, the Lord disappeared through the frame of light; and when Artemisia plunged after him, I felt amost as if we were falling into an ocean of green light.

Everything in front of and around me seemed

to be green. Tall trees soared upward for some fifty meters before they spread out their branches. The thick canopy of green leaves stirred in some distant, high breeze like the surface of a sea; and they filtered the light so that it fell murky and green to the forest floor.

But it was hard to see even the trunks of the trees because vines wound their way around the trunks like green-scaled snakes, and small, shallow-rooted trees grew on the branches and root tops. And where there weren't any trees, there were featherlike ferns some two meters high and humps of moss and lichen. And the air, still and unmoving under the forest top, was heavy and muggy and colored green like the water at the bottom of a still pool.

"The Green Darkness," I murmured as I rose into the air. Almost instantly I felt a twinge from the reopened wounds in my wings.

"Yes." Monkey leapt down nimbly to the forest floor. He sank almost ankle-deep in the old leaves that carpeted the ground. Sweeping off his cap, he gave a deep bow. "My thanks to you, Lord."

The Lord smiled grimly. "You could thank me best by calling on someone else next time that you need help."

Eager to resume my proper size, I touched my forehead and worked the spell that would make me grow again. By that time, the others had dismounted along with the cauldron and Civet. When he had made sure that everything was ready, the Lord brought his horse around.

"Lord." I bowed to him.

When I looked up again, I saw that he was studying me intently; and I felt worse than when the Lady Francolin had inspected me. She had only been measuring me against the heroes of the past; but the Lord seemed to be weighing and examining my very soul—as if it were some raw gemstone. Finally he gave a curt nod. "You've got the old look to you, all right."

I blinked my eyes. "Lord?"

"Like the Weaver and Calambac." His horse stamped its feet nervously, but he quieted it with a squeeze of his knees. "I've seen them all in my time, but you might be one of the best."

I wagged my head from side to side. "I don't mean to contradict you, Lord, but you can't mean me. I've been terrible as a princess."

"I know quite well what I mean. Do you think that Calambac or the Weaver always knew the right thing to do? Half the time they were guessing." He started to swing his horse away but looked over his shoulder with a slight smile. "Just be careful, Your Highness. Monkey has never been known for his caution. Nor has he been noted for his honesty."

"I always keep my word," Monkey protested; but when the Lord looked at him sternly, he added weakly, "most of the time."

The Lord raised his hand to me. "Remember, Your Highness. Sometimes the worst curse is to find your dream."

"And sometimes not," I countered boldly.

"But I think I'm more often right than not." Pulling at his horse's reins, the Lord wheeled round, raising a small cloud of dirt and broken bits of leaf. Artemisia raised a small curved horn and blew three long, descending notes that were as mellow as polished gold. And that strange, brightly colored company followed its somber lord back through the blue hole.

The blue light wavered for a moment and then collapsed together with such a rush that a wind shook the ferns and carpet of leaves. And then the point of light winked out and we were alone within the Green Darkness.

Thorn took the breathing pearl from around his neck. "Well, I'm grateful for the lift; but I can't say that I'm sorry to see them go."

Monkey squatted down beside Civet and examined the bit of chain that had popped out of her mouth. "Yes, none of them is the sort that you would invite for tea and a chat. I was just glad that they were on my side for once." Taking the final link of the chain between his fingertips, Monkey said, "Change!" and the next moment the chain had turned into a hair that he triumphantly restored to his tail.

Thorn tucked the breathing pearl into a little pouch that was hung around his neck. "We promised to return the hair to you."

"And that you did." As a precaution, Monkey took his needle from behind his ear and made it grow into an iron rod. Then he rested the fingertips of his free paw against Civet's temple. When he raised his paw the next moment, Civet's eyes fluttered open.

She lay there for a moment, staring up at the glittering green surface of the forest top. And then she threw up her arms in fear and gave a terrified cry.

I rested a paw on her shoulder. "Easy. You're all right now."

Civet slowly lowered her arms, and I saw not the witch who had lived hundreds of years, but the child she had been before being sacrificed to the river god so long ago. "I thought I was drowning again."

"No, you're in the forest." I smiled as pleasantly as I could and indicated the trees.

"Forest." She blinked her eyes and then put her hands to her stomach. "The chain's gone." She rolled her head to the side so she could look at the forest. "For a moment, I almost thought I was home."

Indigo took her own breathing pearl from around her neck. "You're from the Green Darkness too?"

Civet passed a hand over her face. "No, our forest had pine trees. It's just the light."

"Yes." Indigo nodded her head eagerly. "It's like being in the heart of a giant emerald—just like my parents said it would be."

Civet tried to sit up, but she was still too weak, so I put my paw beneath her back for support and helped raise her. She looked around regretfully. "It wouldn't be such a bad place to live."

I leaned my head to the side. It had been a blessing in disguise to have to escort Indigo here. I looked at her now. "Do you think your people would mind if someone else settled in their forest?"

Indigo stowed her breathing pearl away inside her sack of provisions. "I can't speak for my clan; but I don't see why not. The forest seems big enough."

Civet's eyes darted suspiciously between me and Indigo. "Don't toy with me. I know you've got a cell ready for me in some dungeon."

"I'm more interested in restoring my home." I lifted my paw away.

Civet wrapped her arms around herself. "I told you that I used up most of my magic already. I can't bring your sea back to its old site."

I sighed. "At this point, I'd settle for your promise to help me in whatever way you can."

Civet drew her eyebrows together and stared at me for a long time. "You'd take my word?"

I crouched down so we could look at one another on the same eye level. "You were angry over losing your home so you wanted revenge. I can understand that. Now that I've found my people, I want to give them a home again."

Civet patted the forest floor. "And afterward, you'd let me come back here?"

I nodded my head gravely. "Yes—provided that Indigo's clan agrees."

Civet clapped her hand over one of my forepaws. "Then it's a bargain."

Considering the circumstances, Indigo had been remarkably patient. "Well, I'd like to stand here the rest of the day and make farewell speeches, but I really ought to be getting home." Her face broke into a broad smile at the last word.

"Home is a magical word, isn't it?" I laughed. She was going to find her home sooner than I was, but after almost sacrificing herself for a clan she hardly knew, I think she deserved it.

She'd already taken two steps away from us in her impatience. "I just hope you and your clan know the feeling soon."

In the meantime, Monkey had changed his iron rod back to the size of a needle. "You might as well meet your future neighbors." Putting a paw beneath Civet's elbow, he helped her to her feet.

"But do they want to meet me?" Civet took a rather shaky step with Monkey's help.

"The Kingfisher clan always welcomes everyone." Monkey smacked his lips. "I can just taste those honey cakes now."

Indigo was taking long strides now. "I think we're in the hills to the west of the village," she began to bubble. "If that's true, all we have to do is find Ribbon Creek and follow it downstream to my village."

As we walked along through the thick forest, the excited Indigo turned into a regular chatterbox as she repeated her parents' reminiscences. Once she almost ran into a tree, another time into a tall shrub.

Poor child. I don't think she'd ever had an audience for all of her stories. "You wouldn't know it, but there are beehives up above us." She flung a hand upward toward the thick canopy of leaves overhead. "And up there are also all sorts of orchids and other flowers; so the bees make the sweetest, most fragrant honey." She looked over her shoulder as she shoved through a bush. "You've got to be sure to have a taste—" She frowned when she saw our expressions. "What's wrong?"

Thorn pointed. "The forest . . . It's gone."

"That's impossible," Indigo insisted, and she twisted around to look at the devastated slopes where there were only a few lone tree stumps. Everywhere we looked, the rains had washed away the unrooted soil so that there was only a hard, barren claylike ground that was gullied like the scarred hide of a veteran.

She gave a high, thin wail as if her soul were being burned away like a morning mist. "No, it's not supposed to be like this."

CHAPTER TWENTY-TWO

Before we left the forest's edge, Monkey and I took the precaution of changing ourselves into a middle-aged man and woman. Then, with a new sense of urgency, we marched down the hard, rocky slope. Below us, on the more level areas of the peninsula, we could see the outlines of fields; but the dikes that acted as boundaries and paths had begun to crumble into the weed-filled fields.

"What's wrong?" Thorn whispered to me. "It looks like a wasteland."

I shook my head. "I don't know. It wasn't like this when I came through."

"Maybe they're just letting the fields lie fallow." Indigo broke into a stumbling run that sent her plunging down the slope; and her momentum carried her halfway across one of the fields as dust rose in a cloud behind her.

Civet looked around with sad familiarity. "They've stripped the forest from the slopes and overworked the fields. Erosion's worn away most of the good topsoil; and where it hasn't, the soil's been exhausted."

Bewildered, Indigo whirled around, raising more dust in the process. "How could they let this happen?" she panted to us.

We wound single file along the dike that surrounded the field in which Indigo stood. "I'm sure there's a good explanation for all this," I tried to reassure her.

"There had better be." Swinging around, Indigo began to walk with great, worried strides until she was ahead of us on the dike. And she didn't slow her pace, though twice she slipped on the crumbling footing.

As we turned onto a broad dirt path, we could see the sea in the distance. It looked so cool and inviting that I wished I could run back to it and plunge into the water once again. But of course that was impossible. Instead, we just had to plod along the hot, dusty road. And all the time I could only watch helplessly as Indigo's back stiffened and her hands clenched into fists. This was one fight where her tongue and her fists wouldn't help her.

We didn't see anyone until we were actually within sight of Indigo's village. The bamboo wall around the village had fallen in parts and had not been repaired so we could see how seedy the houses looked. The walls were collapsing and the thatched roofs had holes. It was as if no one cared; or if they did, they didn't have the energy to do anything about it.

The fields held mostly old men and women scratching at the soil with hoes. Their patched tunics and kilts sagged around their bony frames as if they were slowly starving to death.

Indigo broke into a run toward the nearest person—an old man who was tending a field of taro roots. His hair had once been done up in the same blue spikes as the girl, but the dye and grease had worn away so that his spikes drooped sadly. "What's going on?" she demanded.

The old man slowly straightened and blinked his rheumy eyes at her. "Who are you?"

"Joy and Increase's daughter," she said desperately.

The old man wrinkled his forehead as if he were

having trouble recalling the names. "Are you sure they were from the Kingfisher clan?"

"My father was the chief. He led the protest against the Butcher." Indigo slapped her hands against her legs in exasperation. "You couldn't have forgotten him already."

The old man scratched his cheek. "But that was so long ago. And so many others have run away or died or been taken . . ." His voice drifted away absently.

But in the meantime other old people had left their fields to see what the commotion was all about. "Yes"—a tiny old woman shook her finger thoughtfully at Indigo—"you have Joy's persistence."

Indigo clutched at the old woman's arm. "They told me all about our home—the forests, the fields, the singing, the laughing."

"That was before the Butcher came and took away the young folk to build his forts." She turned and spat toward the foot of the peninsula where a large wooden fort perched above the sea. "And he had the trees cut down from the hills because he needed ships for his great war with the dragons."

"I hope the dragons gobble him up," another old man swore.

The old woman made hushing motions to him as a middle-aged man with a wooden peg leg stumped up. She nodded toward him as if she were afraid of having him overhear more. Could he be an informer?

But Indigo was beyond noticing as she collapsed to her knees. "How could you let him do this to my home. How?"

The first old man slowly raised his shoulders as if he barely had the energy for that gesture and then he lowered them. "We had no choice."

And all I could think of were the words of the Lord of Flowers: that the worst curse was to find your dreams. Things didn't seem to be turning out the way Indigo had expected. "It'll be all right, child," I tried to soothe her.

Indigo clawed up a handful of dirt and flung it into the air. "But you don't understand. Home is what kept me going."

I tried to think of something comforting to say, but, much to my surprise, it was Civet who spoke first.

"I know that dream," she said quietly. "I came

home only to find that it had been turned into a wasteland."

"And so do I," I added.

Civet rounded on her heel to face me. "Yes, of course." And I saw that she finally understood what she had done to my clan when she had stolen our sea. In an odd sort of way, it gave us a common bond. "I'm sorry for what I did to you and your clan."

It might not have satisfied Sergeant Chukar or the Lady Francolin, but it was a start and so that was enough for me. "That's in the past now. Let's see what we can do about keeping it from happening again."

Civet put a protective hand on Indigo's shoulder. "At least not to her."

Indigo just started shaking her head. "It's not fair. It's just not fair. I did what I was supposed to do. My home should have been waiting for me."

I cupped Indigo's chin and forced her to look up at me. "Remember what Lady Francolin said about dragon steel. You're being tempered for just a little longer."

Indigo pulled free. "But for what?" she demanded miserably.

Thorn, who had been carrying the cauldron, set it down on the ground and wagged a finger at her. "Stop carrying on like that. Restoring a village will be child's play next to bringing back a whole sea."

Indigo sat back on her heels. "You'd help me?"

"You've proved yourself." Thorn impulsively sat on the edge of the cauldron. "In fact, I think you belong on our team."

Indigo wiped a tear clumsily from her eyes as if she hadn't had much practice at that sort of thing. "I thought that you didn't want another person hanging around."

Thorn gave me a questioning look; and when I nodded my head, he turned back to Indigo with a broad grin. "I think our partnership is big enough for more than two people."

"Especially when it's someone like you," I agreed.

I was glad when Indigo straightened up a little. "Well," she admitted, "maybe dreams are like people. They have to be tempered too."

Thorn pantomimed walking with two of his fingers. "Then you'll come with us?"

Indigo gave a little toss of her head. "I'd hate to think of you two stumbling around without me."

Suddenly a deep boom sounded from the distant fort. The vibrations seemed to travel through the very ground to tingle our toes. A second boom followed and then a third in a deep, heavy rhythm— as if there were a giant frog underneath our feet puffing itself up and thumping away.

Thorn jumped up startled. "What's that?"

I looked to the fort. "War drums. The humans and the dragons have started the biggest foolishness of all."

"That's just great," Indigo blurted out and her voice cracked in exasperation. "Things were going to be hard enough for us already without a war."

I turned to Indigo. She was doing her best to hold back her tears while all those old folk stared at her so curiously. "We'll worry about mending the cauldron first; and then we'll tackle our other problems." I didn't say any more because the peg-legged man had edged in closer.

In the meantime, though, Indigo's eyes searched my face. "How are you going to do all that?"

I shook out a kink in my shoulder. "I know a smith who might repair the cauldron. And as for the rest, we'll manage to find a way."

Thorn grinned at her encouragingly. "After all,

we've managed to come this far. we just need to go a little farther."

"I guess we have." The corners of Indigo's mouth twitched up cautiously; and I took that for a good sign. "And I guess we will."

But we would all need to be like dragon steel now.

Laurence Yep grew up in San Francisco, where he was born. He attended Marquette University, was graduated from the University of California at Santa Cruz, and received his Ph.D. from the State University of New York at Buffalo.

His novel DRAGONWINGS was a Newbery Honor Book of 1976, an ALA Notable Children's Book of 1975, and the recipient of the International Reading Association's 1976 Children's Book Award. His other titles include SWEETWATER, CHILD OF THE OWL, SEA GLASS, DRAGON OF THE LOST SEA, KIND HEARTS AND GENTLE MONSTERS, and THE SERPENT'S CHILDREN.